JOURNEY *to* SYCHAR

Valdene Williams

ISBN 979-8-89243-031-9 (paperback)
ISBN 979-8-89243-032-6 (digital)

Copyright © 2024 by Valdene Williams

All rights reserved. No part of this publication may be reproduced, distributed, or transmitted in any form or by any means, including photocopying, recording, or other electronic or mechanical methods without the prior written permission of the publisher. For permission requests, solicit the publisher via the address below.

Christian Faith Publishing
832 Park Avenue
Meadville, PA 16335
www.christianfaithpublishing.com

Printed in the United States of America

Part 1

CHAPTER 1

A single rooster call began each day, and each morning, the same rooster made the same sound, as if he was giving a warning of the approaching dawn to the occupants of the slave huts he faced. It was still dark in the hut where the girl slept, but the moonlight shone through the cracks of the shack, falling on her where she lay on her palette.

Penda opened her eyes as she heard praying. She recognized some of the words as they were like the prayers of her parents to their gods who covered the tabletop in their hut. The list of names connected to each hut was called, and prayers for their safety and strength were offered. Penda, the girl, sat up when she heard, "God grant Sarah strength to carry out her duties, give her favor with Mistress Mapp. Help her to know that thou can do it. Let all de promises of dis Bible be real to her and may all de children of de plantation come to know you and be obedient. As Abraham's son Isaac was yours, Isaac's Jacob was loved by you, and Jacob's son Joseph found favor in your sight, God please do for all these men, women, and children here at Coconut Palms as thou hast done for your people a long time ago, and, God, help all de slaves to be free one day, amen."

Penda had been ordered by Master Mapp to live with the old woman known as Mammy. She made prayer and Bible reading at 4:00 a.m., a daily ritual, and continued until the first signs of daylight, when the roll call was completed, and the slaves headed out to the sugarcane fields.

Master Mapp was overheard by his houseboy making plans to have a girl trained by Mammy in roots, herbs, and delivery of babies.

"I have watched Mammy's decline with her advancing years, and I know that it is only a matter of a few years before she will no longer be capable or able to deliver and care for babies. Sarah seems the most likely to be taught, being young and according to mistress Catherine has shown quickness in learning new skills in the big house as well as in English.

When the girl met Mammy, she thought she saw a resemblance to her grandmother, and she spoke slowly like her.

Outside Mammy's hut was a fireplace where all her cooking was done. In the hut, a palette made from dried grass was stuffed into a large pillowcase of rice bags that were sewn together and placed on the mud floor, a common practice in her village. There were tree stumps outside the hut where Mammy's visitors would sit. The outline of her duties was given by Master Mapp. "You will help Mammy until noon, after which you will go to the big house to wait on Mistress Catherine. She usually sleeps until that time."

"Yessuh," the girl answered.

Mammy's hut looked different from the other huts. It was made of wood, but her roof looked like all the others, covered with broad leaves from the plantain tree.

Sarah, her plantation name under Mammy, learned the herbs used for treating all kinds of ailments, and she accompanied her to learn the art of delivering babies.

Every day Penda thought of escaping Coconut Palms plantation, with many hours spent fine-tuning and examining the what-ifs of running away. All plans of escape were worked through with Kuba, a young man from her village who also wanted to run away. The day finally came when their plan was firmly in place. They would leave close to the end of a workday when all the slaves and overseers would be busy. However, there were some unanswered questions that brought a cloud of fear. Where would they go? There had been rumors of runaways at Saint John, the adjacent parish. How far was it? Could they leave the island? If yes, would they not need a canoe or a boat? What could happen to them if they were caught? To the last question, Kuba said he would kill himself before the overseer could.

JOURNEY TO SYCHAR

What crippled the girl were the memories of the night her village was captured. The fresh images of that night and the experience of the slave ship she rehearsed and relived constantly until she eventually gave up all ideas of running away.

CHAPTER 2

Captain Clarke was a regular visitor to the village of Lunda because of its proximity to water. On a couple of occasions, he brought gifts that were exchanged for elephant tusks. On the day of capture, news went out that the village was invited to see his new boat. There was also a rumor that people from her village had left to work at the river but never returned. Many of the elders refused to believe it. On hearing the words *not come back* spoken repeatedly, Clarke quickly changed the invitation to a party in the village square. Everyone except the older men went. Penda and her family arrived after most of the surrounding villages had started eating and dancing to the beat of the drums. The atmosphere was one of gaiety and happiness. Finally exhausted, they made their way back to their respective villages.

The oldest girl, Penda, fourteen, by how many yam harvests had passed since her birth, had just extinguished the lamp and the family had stretched themselves out on their mats when they were awakened by a loud commotion. Blinding flashlights were shone around the hut and in their faces. The girl tried to stand but her legs felt weak. After a few attempts, she pushed herself up from the mat as shouts and screams seemed to come closer and louder. A hand was held tightly over her mouth preventing her from screaming.

She caught sight of her mother and father as the light swept around the room. Her mother was crying holding her younger brother. Noises of loud crying, gasps and screams were heard coming from everywhere outside along with the sound of running feet and another sound she learned later came from chains.

The whole village was rounded up by two burly-looking men and made to assemble in one long line on the path outside the huts. They were shouting words that no one understood. Anyone who offered resistance was roughly pushed, slapped, and beaten into compliance.

The men of the village were connected by chains around their necks. Some could be heard pleading to their gods for help, while others fought and struggled to free themselves, eventually giving up as being overpowered they recognized the futility of their struggle.

The women and children were lined up in single file next to two men who were holding what looked like broomsticks. As a long rope was tied tightly around their waists and wrists women could be heard in their dialects pleading with the men to take them but let the children go. In response to their pleadings, they were pushed and shoved down the dirt track that led away from the village.

As they stood on the track weeping, they were blinded by flashlights being deliberately shone in their eyes. A long rope was wound and knotted so tightly around their right wrists that any jerking movement would have torn the skin. Tears flowed as they walked. Sometimes the captives would hear the crack of a whip and moaning coming from behind them, but they knew not to look back.

They walked through the night until dawn signaled a new day. In the dim light, Penda looked closely at the rope around her wrists while the reality of her capture and fear of the unknown engulfed her.

The rope around her wrist was linked to the wrist of the person in front and behind her continuing to the end of the line. The sun was rising with intense heat when one of their captors moved to the back of the line. Penda glanced quickly behind her, she noticed blood running down the forehead and right cheek of the woman walking directly behind her. Thankfully she could see that the eye was spared. As the sun reached overhead, Penda became conscious of the rope cutting into her skin and the profuse sweating and odor of herself and the women around her.

Suddenly the woman walking in front of Penda fell forward to the ground, pulling everyone behind her in line forward. It was then Penda noticed that her back was bleeding profusely.

"Get up!" a man's voice shouted, but the woman remained still.

"Get up!" he shouted again. After the line of captives had regained their balance, he kicked the woman, but she did not move. The man then removed the rope from her waist and wrist, dragged her body to the side of the track, and ordered everyone to keep walking.

The captives walked on until a stop was made for them to toilet, get water, and for their captors who were visibly exhausted from the heat to take a brief rest. Many of them were unable to drink when water from the stream was given to them as their tongues had become swollen from thirst and heat.

They were forced to walk along again this time at a very rapid pace. The group was smaller as men and women were dying daily. Those who died, their bodies were left at the side of the track, others were alive but too weak to continue the journey and suffered the same fate. After many days and nights of walking through the heat, rain, and cold, they came to a large body of water. They were hungry and thirsty. Their feet were scorched, swollen, and bleeding. Many begged to be left alone to die. The walk reminded Penda in some ways of going to harvest yams with the women of the village when she would become tired, her footsteps would become slower, and she would beg to stop for a rest. Her mother would say, "Walking at a slower pace, does not stop, slow time, or shorten the distance."

As the days wore on, the piercing rays of the sun wearied the captives and slowed progress noticeably. To ease the burning of the sun on her forehead, Penda kept her head down until she noticed a trail of bloody footprints. *Someone ahead of me must have bleeding feet she thought.*

The girl tried assessing her chance of escaping. Could she outrun her captors? Was there a good chance of being free? If there was a sliver of a chance of freedom she would try. Two of the captors moved to the front of the line. She worked the rope around her wrist, down her right hand, and over her fingers. Then she held the rope as if she was still bound by it. Penda was as sure as a fourteen-year-old brain could think that she could outrun her captors once she got into the trees, she could lose them. She took off running as fast as her feet could move, surprising herself.

Within a few steps of the trees and before the captors noticed and gave chase, she stumbled and fell. She couldn't move as the impact of the fall on her weakened body took her breath away. Unable to cry, she looked up into the eyes of a small man whose head looked too big for his body. Dragging her off the ground, the rope was knotted so tightly around her wrists that they became bruised in the process. Foolishly she called on all her gods for help, hoping that they were watching and somehow would intervene.

As the men resumed the walk, ashamed and humiliated at her failure to escape, the girl walked with her head down for the remainder of the journey. After many days and nights of walking, they reached a large river. Many more people had died, and those remaining seemed lifeless. Sitting on the water were large canoes filled with people from various villages identified by their head ties and tribal marks on the women's faces. While Penda and her village waited to be untied there was loud shouting from the people in the first canoes in the water. It didn't take long for the people to figure out the warning being shouted. "Fight and run, no work, straw man fooled us!" This was shouted over and over.

In the commotion, the filled canoes were rowed quickly downstream by two men whose skins were blackened. The first canoe rounded a bend quickly and was lost from view. Overwhelmed, the girl looked around frantically searching in the sea of faces for her parents.

A net was thrown over them as men, women, and children were pushed into the second empty canoe which moved slowly downstream, rowed by four men. She didn't recognize them from her village because their dialect was unfamiliar to her. She had never been on the river before and feared that at the edge of the water, the canoe would fall over an edge. By midday of the first day, the sun was now directly overhead. The sun beat down on them without mercy, but evening and night brought a welcome coolness. During the evening and the stillness of the night, the men continued to row. The only sound that broke the night was the sound of the water against the paddles.

Then suddenly she was snatched out of her meditations by shouts of "sea." The shouts were coming from their captors, who seemed excited. To Penda the word 'sea', was strange, but before she could figure out what it meant when the canoe came around a bend, they saw a large collection of water, and sitting on the water were what looked like two gigantic birds with a large white cloth jutting out at the top. These birds were called ships and used for transporting them to a new world. Penda had a brief glimpse of her parents and sisters as they mounted the steps to the big ship after that she never saw them again. The last site she had of her father was that of a shackled man covered by a net being herded onto the first ship.

She had never been to the sea or the river before, but the way the villagers spoke of the river made it seem alive. They rode past the first ship until they came to the second ship. At the second ship, a large net was thrown over them as they were hauled on deck. On the ship, they were assigned places to sit. She identified by their dress the village chiefs, African nobility who were leaders of their villages, and feared witch doctors manacled and forced to sit together in the same place with their nakedness exposed.

Sitting across from the girl Penda was Odon, a boy from her village who was struggling to free himself from the chains, but he was fastened tightly to the man sitting next to him. "We are prisoners," a conclusion the girl reached early as looking around, they had no freedom of movement or privacy to relieve natural body functions. She thought of her maid who was captured by her village during the last war. She thought of the family's gods that she should have brought with her and things that she could have done to avoid recapture. The first night after the ship set sail, no one slept, as everyone was afraid of the unknown. The allotted space on the boat allowed them to sit but not stand or stretch out as every space on the ship was filled with a body; they were shackled together plus the beams were too low to allow standing.

Penda was unable to look at the nakedness of the men and women on the ship as it went against her upbringing, yet she was forced to do so being unable to move from the place to which she was assigned. She felt desperate to have a bath as her head and body itched from the sweat and heat. She looked around at the people sitting opposite, their faces looked haggard, their eyes hollow staring lifelessly back at her. The cries and wailing of the children on the first night became unbearable when their mothers were unable to comfort them. With nowhere to go and nothing to do with their time, they sat confined to one place. Occasionally buckets of water were thrown over them, but it was ineffective in getting rid of the stench that clung to their bodies.

Frequently, the girl's thoughts would turn from the state of things on the ship to fears for her brother who slipped away on the night of the raid. She was thankful that no one seemed to notice him escaping in the confusion. She eventually consoled herself that he is better off than her, wherever he was in the bush.

How long can he survive in the bush? Did he return to the hut hoping they returned? Was he hungry?

Again, she consoled herself. "He was better off than me. He didn't have to walk day and night without food and water or sit tied up on a ship." She pictured him with his red dusty feet and boyish grin, and the tears came.

Days and nights became mixed up, as they had no way of measuring time, so were unable to calculate time spent at sea. People became sick and some died. She watched helpless as unfamiliar hands fondled the women's bodies, dreading the moment she could become an unwilling participant. The captors would choose women, and where they were taken, no one knew. Sometimes they heard screams other times when the women returned there would be bruising on their faces and naked bodies.

As the weeks on the ship passed, Penda heard men and women expressing words that didn't make sense, an indication of them starting to lose their sanity. She heard prominent men like chiefs crying in pain forced to sit close to their servants in their filth. Their moods would change suddenly from singing to crying then anger. Men talked to themselves and cried, and at other times, they became suicidal, attempting to jump overboard. Some attempts were successful. Many expressed being betrayed by the captain who gained their trust with gifts.

The ship was named *God Speed*. Its first stop was a place called Ghana. There, more people were brought on board and crammed into every available space.

Sometime after leaving Ghana, many people along with two of their captors got sick and died.

The cramped conditions, malnutrition, no ventilation, and limited inadequate toilet facilities were believed to be the causes of death. With so many lives lost, the ship was turned back to Ghana where more people were captured to replace the people who died.

Leaving Ghana for the second time, the ship encountered a storm. Penda remembered the ship being tossed about in the sea like a dry twig and the look of fear on everyone's faces.

Each day that passed on the ship, the food given to the captives became inedible and less until there was none. More people, mainly children, died. Sharks followed the ship daily in anticipation of the ready meals that would be thrown at them. Everyone in their tribal dialect could be heard daily, asking the same questions but not expecting answers.

What going to happen to we?

What have my parents or my compound done to be treated like this?

Why was my village captured? Which of de gods we make angry?

How long is de journey? When does it end? Questions were asked by the girl as well as many of the captives but without answers.

To the questions, Penda knew that only their captors knew the destination and the reason they were captured. As the journey continued Penda's emotions mirrored those of the captives on the ship, with fear, confusion, and hopelessness visible on each face.

Escaping the ship alive now seemed impossible, yet one question that haunted her was *why was there no collective effort to fight or resist* since there were four straw-colored men, maybe one more with the captain, and a ship full of men.

She reasoned that beyond the physical impediment of the chains, no one among them would know how to direct the ship back. And without a common language by which to communicate plots and plans any thought of returning to her village was quickly aborted.

Then something changed on the ship. They were being given better food and larger portions. Their bodies were rubbed with oil. Water was thrown over their bodies on a regular basis, in an unsuccessful attempt to wash away weeks of feces and urine, yet the stench on their weak and emaciated bodies remained, the result of prolonged starvation.

After many weeks on the ship, they arrived at a place named Barbados. It was a sunny day with a warm breeze. Men women and the few children who survived the journey got cleaned up. Cold water was thrown over their bodies, and then they were lined up and led onto a platform facing a table where four serious-looking men sat staring at them as they walked down the gangplank. One of the men paraded one of the women, then he pried open her mouth to show her teeth. Babies born on the ship were held in their mother's arms. Penda was still unable to look around at the naked bodies being displayed.

Unkind eyes looked at their naked bodies as men and women were physically examined by prospective buyers. Humiliated and embarrassed, Penda tried covering her private parts with her hands until one of the men said, laughing, "This one doesn't know her body is not hers."

Perceived prospective buyers walked up and down in front of them, feeling their muscles, making audible judgments on the state of their health and morality, some even conversed with them maybe to discover what degree of intelligence and docility they possessed. The sight of their emaciated bodies brought no looks of sympathy from the men. Instead, it seemed to increase levity and pleasure at their misery and fear. After what seemed like a large exchange of words, a clear sound of one word *sold* was shouted repeatedly as each captive was unchained. The whole experience was terrifying for them, as they had no idea of what fate awaited them.

"A strong healthy buck, good for the field no defects, no less than one hundred pounds."

"This one here will be good for the house and cooking fifty pounds."

When they came to Odon, one of the men, laughing and pointing at him, said, "This one is perfect for my house. He will make the perfect house servant." Pointing to Kuba and Penda, he said, "This boy will be good for the field. He will be a great breeder of sons, and the girl will be a mother of many strong sons. I'll take these three for one hundred pounds!" shouted one man.

"One hundred pounds is the starting price!" shouted a man who was holding a hammer.

Kuba was naked, and he stood towering over the auctioneer and guards while his skin glistened from the oil rub on the ship.

There was silence, then whispers among the men.

The three of them were prodded, pulled, and inspected for physical disabilities. When Penda's turn came, she was led onto the platform from where she looked down at a group of faces staring at her.

A man and a woman standing directly below the platform seemed engaged in a discussion glancing occasionally at Penda.

"I think it's a bargain. I think that tall one is worth that by himself," the man said.

Someone shouted out 240 pounds, and the offer was repeated by the man with the hammer. Then someone shouted 350 pounds. The man with the hammer repeated the same.

"Gentlemen, what do I hear?" Silence, then the hammer came down on the stone.

"For 350 pounds—final." She was stunned for a moment until she was startled by a different voice. Turning to look, Penda observed the voice came from a black man who seemed to appear out of nowhere. He was tall and bent over, and when he walked, he rocked from side to side.

"Come wid me," the voice said, making a motion with his hand. "My name is Bassa. I oversee what goes on at de plantation."

They followed him past the holding pen where the rest of the slaves from the ship stood waiting.

Bassa took Kuba into a shack by the docks, and there two men put chains on him. Then a hot iron with a number was stamped on Kuba and Odon's back. They were both silent during the ordeal, but Penda was not stamped. The branding would, in the future, become a daily reminder that they were not people with an identity but things to be used and abused at their owner's will.

On hearing the three of them speak his tribal dialect, the man knew that they were from his village. Fearing they could be sold, he threatened them with whippings if he ever heard them speaking that language again.

"English is the language of dis plantation," he said. Now not only were their names changed, but also they were prohibited from speaking in their native tongue and lost a fundamental right, the ability to communicate.

They waited on the wharf for their master and mistress, Matthew and Catherine Mapp, who arrived with two other servants. No one seemed to care about their emotional trauma or cultural disorientation that they had suffered being snatched from their homes. Instead, they were immediately stripped of their tribal names, identities, and religion. Kuba was renamed Absalom, Penda's was named Sarah, and Odon was Philemon. Now not only were their names changed, but also they were prohibited from speaking their native tongue. They would later learn that this was a common practice on the plantation aimed at inducing quick amnesia of their identities.

Thinking of the new names Penda reflected on the naming ceremony in her village. It was a celebration with special meaning. She was taught that a name was a verbal symbol of one's identity and position in the family and village community. Her ancestors believed that to separate a person from their name was to destroy the core of who they were. She didn't know the meaning of her new name Sarah, but she knew that Penda means loved, Kuba means "the holder of the heel," and Odon "prosperous protection." If given the name of a recently deceased relative it was believed that the baby would inherit that person's strengths or weaknesses.

When Penda saw Master Mapp, her first emotion was fear. He was straw-colored like her captors, the men who pinched her breasts, examined her body, and burnt their backs with hot irons. He was tall with straw-colored hair. He had a large nose and a wide mouth that was shaded by thick hair on his top lip. His head was high, and his head seemed too big for his neck and body. A woman followed him who the girl supposed was his wife.

The walk from the wharf in Bridgetown to Coco Palms plantation in Saint Philip was accompanied by Bassa and drivers, Chibone and Philip. As newly purchased slaves, they were forced to trudge the thirty miles from Saint Michael to the plantation on foot over hills and bad roads. They arrived exhausted but with enough light to see people who bore a resemblance in color to themselves. One could see that there was a marked disparity in their ages; they were either much older or very young.

The path leading to their huts was narrow and slippery with overgrown brush and twisted vines.

After the ship journey and the long walk, the girl and her friends were happy to be horizontal. As she lay down, she made herself remember her sisters and brothers, the conversations they would have before sleep, as well as day-to-day events in the village. She thought of her brother, and sisters Makena and Kanoni.

"Selling my good servants de same as selling my children," Penda's father was speaking to someone at the front of their hut. "Are you asking me to sell my servants?"

"No, suh," Penda recognized the voice of Teggah.

Their village knew that he was shifty and made a living from trickery and deceptive practices. Teggah had a deep gaping wound on his face that made him look as if he was always smiling. The wound ran down his right lip, preventing his mouth from closing, and his right eye looked bigger than the left, and the lid kept open from the scar.

The evening before the capture, he had visited their village with a man whose hair was straw colored and moved when the wind blew.

Her father was sitting on a tree stump at the front of their hut, a common practice of the older men while the girls and their mothers cooked supper on the fireplace at the back.

"Only two?" an unfamiliar voice asked.

"Ah no, you see odders after we talk in de hut," Teggah answered.

"Make we go inside ba." A request was made by Teggah to the older man.

"Penda, come get the man a drink," her father requested.

"Yes, ba," her response barely audible above the noise of the compound.

She understood words of the conversation like *money, pay*, "I bring dem" in bits of their dialect. On bringing the drink, Penda observed the man's face closely.

The man looked angry while her father was silent. After a few mins, he walked off in the direction of the pond, leaving Teggah who was visibly disappointed, and ran behind him, shouting, "Wait!"

A word the girl did not understand.

She dozed but woke up several times during the night disoriented, tearful, and afraid. She awoke the next morning while it was still dark feeling tired as if she had not slept. They had been shown the latrines yesterday, made from a hole in the ground with two planks laid across set a little distance away from the huts. She got off the mat, walked to the door of the hut, looked outside but seeing no movement, she reluctantly returned to lie down unable to sleep. While she waited for daylight, she heard a baby crying. The sound came from a hut on the right accompanied by loud snoring like her father did after a long hunt. She walked toward the crying hoping the snoring was her father since she was unable to ignore the sound or fall back asleep.

Penda walked and listened until the sound was located. She lifted the burlap door covering and stepped into the hut. Sitting on the floor in the semidarkness was an old woman holding a baby. A kerosene lamp next to her on the floor gave just enough light for the girl to see the woman and make out the form of a man whose face was turned away. When their eyes met in the dim light, Penda saw a look of raw terror on the woman's face and in her eyes. The woman made hand gestures to her that initially she did not understand but interpreted them to mean get out of here quickly before he woke up. The woman kept pointing to the man, then to the girl and the door.

There was something about the woman's attitude that made the girl obey her gestures. She left quickly and went back to her hut to await the morning and the beginning of her life on Coconut Palms plantation. Without any announcement, scalding hot tears flowed down her cheeks, and she didn't try to stop them, nor wipe them away.

Instead, pretended that her mother's arms were wrapped around her, and then she froze as she heard a sound like that of a night animal.

A conch shell horn blew just before dawn that first morning and every day except Sunday. Someone was shouting repeatedly, "Get out! Out!" These are the first English words Penda learned. As she came out of her hut, she hesitated for a second because the man doing the shouting was Bassa the Overseer who collected them from the wharf the day before, and she believed he was the snoring man in the hut. Penda noted he wore a shirt, pants, and shoes while the men were naked from the waist up, and the women wore a loose coarse covering. He moved slowly as he walked through the line that morning at roll call just staring at them. Penda could hear her friend Odon breathing heavily while his body trembled under the overseer's stares.

The men, children, and women were quickly assembled and sent off to the fields. The three new slaves. Penda, Odon, and Kuba were asked to gather in the common area for the reading of the laws which were read to all new slaves on their first day. Master Mapp had a paper in his hand from which he was reading.

Each runaway slave shall lose one leg, or if pardoned by me shall be given fifty lashes.

Any slave aware of the intention of slaves to run away and withhold such information shall be burned on the forehead and given fifty lashes.

Those who inform me of a slave's plans to run away shall receive a reward.

A slave who runs away and returns after eight days shall receive fifty lashes a week for eight weeks unless pardoned by the governor.

Anyone who steals and is caught shall be pinched with hot pincers and receive one hundred lashes.

Slaves who receive stolen goods or protect runaways shall be branded and given as many lashes as determined by the governor.

A slave who strikes a white man or woman shall lose his hand.

The practice of witchcraft shall be punished by flogging.

A slave who attempts to poison his master or mistress shall be pinched with hot pincers three times and then be broken on a wheel.

A free slave who harbors a slave or thief shall lose his freedom.

All dances, feasts, and plays are forbidden unless permission is obtained from the master or overseer.

No slave can marry without the master's consent.

Slaves are not to look their master or mistress in the eye. Eyes must be cast down or to the side.

A slave who strikes an overseer, master, or mistress shall lose their hand.

Slaves can be bought, sold, or given away at the will of the master.

What seemed strange was they were expected to understand words written in English that they had never heard or spoken before.

"How could I be obedient when I don't understand?" the girl asked herself. "Obedience could only come from the fear of the whip," she reasoned.

Then Master Mapp, speaking as if his nose was stuffed, said, "You will start in the field tomorrow. Bassa the overseer will give you orders."

CHAPTER 3

From Penda's observations of her first week in the field, children aged six to twelve were assigned lighter fieldwork like pulling weeds or gathering grass. Women mainly worked in the fields while men did most of the skilled jobs like carpentry and operating the sugar mill under supervision.

Workdays were from dawn until dark six days a week and varied according to the amount of daylight, as well as according to the attitude of the master or overseer, as well as times of planting and harvesting. Sundays were excluded.

On Penda's first day in the field, she was assigned to the weeders group.

"Your job is to pull up de weeds from round de baby sugarcane cause dey hide mice!" Bassa shouted.

Cleaning and weeding were done three times during the growth of sugarcane. Her first day was spent digging out unwanted weeds or pulling them up by hand.

Two men stood behind the workers, making sure they worked quickly. They carried long whips that made a noise before it landed on the bare backs or heads of the workers. There seemed to be a sequence of steps in the preparation and maneuvering of the soil, the planting of the sugarcane, and the weeding and harvesting. Planting and harvesting were matched with the rainy and dry seasons. Machetes and cutlasses were used to chop the sugarcane close to the ground the leaves were stripped then the plant would be cut into short pieces three or four feet in length and bundles of the cane would then be carried to the mills by slaves or in carts pulled by a mule.

By midmorning of Penda, Odon, and Kuba's first day in the field with the sun high overhead and the heat intense they were given water by two small houseboys. The sun was hotter than anything she remembered in the hottest month of Lunda. After five days in the sun, fearing that she would collapse from the work and the sweltering heat, Mistress Mapp asked her husband to bring Penda into the house as one of her personal slaves. She assigned her to work with Deborah, another house slave who was instructed to teach Penda everything she had been taught.

How can I tell them of my inability to understand or speak English? the girl fretted.

The next morning, she woke up sore from having to bend constantly pulling weeds, her fingers had many tiny cuts, and her feet were covered in blisters from the hot earth.

There was a sequence of steps in preparing Penda to be Catherine's personal servant. First mistress had the doctor examine her for the presence of sores, fever, or deformities. Next, she had to be trained by the senior house servant, Chibone. He was tall with white hair and very black skin. His back was stooped, and he walked very slowly. Deborah, the house servant chosen to train the girl, looked older, judging from her white hair under the head wrap. Penda hoped that the other house slaves would remember their first weeks on the plantation and would show kindness to her.

"I been many years on dis plantation, and I serve Master Mapp's father," Chibone told the girl with a stern face. "Listen and do as I say, and you be alright. Speak only when Mistress or Master speaks to you. Always go in the house through de back entrance, dat way for servants, front stairs for Master's friends. Ask me or Timothy if you don't know wat to do. You help cook in de kitchen till Mistress sends for you." She was then dismissed to the kitchen for her duties.

The first night at the plantation, Odon and Kuba slept well on their mats. Kuba's body hurt from the bending and stooping. The prolonged cramped position on the ship added to the discomfort. He was angry at being tricked by one of his village men, Teggah. The hot brand stamped on his back was still burning while the heat from the sun intensified the pain. He reviewed his first day in the field, the thirst, the hunger, the overseer shouting sounds he could not understand.

Dazed from the heat, he gestured to the man on the row next to him that he was hungry and thirsty. Turning around, he came face-to-face with the overseer, Bassa, who shouted some words to him. After much gesturing, Kuba understood he was to wait for the water boy who would come once a day with a large can from which he filled a small cup once for each slave. Some days when ugly moods controlled the overseers the slaves got nothing. To ask for more than one cup was seen as idling and could be rewarded with a whip across the back. Putting down his bag of sugarcane seedlings Kuba crossed the field and faced Bassa.

In his native dialect, he said, "De people need water and food, dey sick and will die."

Their eyes met for a few seconds. Kuba waited for the whip in Bassa's hand to land on his body. Instead, Bassa looked away and answered him yes, while Kuba turned away silently, walked back to the group, and resumed planting. Bassa understood Kuba as they were from the same village.

For the rest of the week, Bassa treated Kuba with a reluctant respect because he could not deny that the boy worked harder and faster than the other field hands. He was watched closely after a conversation with Bassa and Master Mapp was overheard.

"That new boy, Absalom, must be watched. I see him arranging the slaves. He put weak ones and dem little children in between two people to help dem catch up."

"Yes, watch him," Mapp answered.

What Master and Bassa did not know was Kuba was teaching the field hands how to avoid a beating.

Kuba woke up the second day with a start. Confused and disoriented in time and place, he asked out loud, "Where am I?" as daylight was forcing its way through the cracks of the hut. On blistered feet, he hobbled past the burlap blind and out into the open air to await his assignment.

There was a big storm one night that happened about one sugarcane harvest after the three friends' arrival on the plantation. First, there was a flash of lightning followed by a loud clap of thunder. The noise of the rain beating on the roof of the hut sounded like someone was throwing stones. At other times the wind sounded like screams. Other times noises of bumping thumping, crashing, and banging, reviving the fears the girl had experienced the night of her capture. A heavy sleep must have edged its way into her thoughts as unaware of the wind dying down, she eventually fell into a deep sleep. She was awoken suddenly by the sound of something snapping.

Must be Master Mapp cracking his whip, she thought. He was coming along the path leading to her group of huts. This had become his custom every night since several slaves had run away from the surrounding plantations and were camped out at Bagatelle nearby. She thought that Master Mapp maybe did this in the hopes of scaring any of his slaves who might be tempted to join the runaways. The sounds kept coming closer until the footsteps stopped briefly outside her hut, then resumed until they stopped next to her body on the mat inside the hut.

Her body began to tremble uncontrollably fearing what he might do to her. She kept her eyes closed pretending to be asleep, hoping that he would leave. She concluded from the overwhelming, unmistakable strong smell of rum that the master was drunk a picture she had seen before.

He shouted her name, drawing it out for a few seconds, "Sarah!"

Even though one harvest had passed, she was still not used to being called Sarah. She wasn't sure if it was more suited to an old woman or an old man. Many times, she had to do a quick reorientation of her name to avoid the whip as silence was taken for insolence.

She remained quiet as her body was nudged a couple of times with his foot attempting to wake her up. The lantern he carried was placed on the ground next to her face.

"Sarah, do you hear me?" Words becoming slurred, almost unintelligible.

It was obvious he had been drinking a lot, and he wanted her awake. He kept nudging her with his foot and pushing the lantern closer until the heat began to burn. She opened her eyes and sat up.

"I hear you, Massuh."

He remained standing while she rose to a standing position and moved a few steps away from the lantern, keeping her eyes cast to the ground as per slave law.

"I want you to know that the laws do not apply to you," he said. "They are meant for the stupid and ungrateful who do not know how good they have it. Do you understand?"

"Yes, suh," she said, not fully understanding.

His tone of voice became sad as he said, "This year has been a very hard year for the plantation. The last hurricane we experienced flattened all the sugarcane. Then before we could catch ourselves, the whole island experienced a severe drought with no rain for months. Because of this, we had a small crop of sugarcane this year, and it gave us a little rum and a little sugar."

For a minute, she tried to understand what he was saying as her English was not good, but his tone of voice was sad.

Never had he talked to her in that manner as to a human being. This was the first time since she had been on the plantation, and this may have been because her time was spent catering to his wife's every need.

"I have tried everything and failed. We feed our slaves. I personally do not whip them, yet they run away. This plantation and all the remaining slaves may be sold if the men and women keep running away."

"Massa, dey want freedom." Penda was surprised at the force with which she spoke having learned just enough English words in six months to patch together some meaning.

His shoulders stiffened, and he hesitated for a few minutes, then he cleared his throat.

"When be that, suh?"

"When you be ready for freedom, I give it."

"I be ready now, suh," Penda spoke, hoping that by sunrise, he would have forgotten this night.

She tried to figure out what his facial expression might have been as she dared not look at his face. Was he puzzled, impatient, or angry? He allowed her to speak for a little while using broken English words mixed with her tribal dialect.

"You be a fadder, suh, please have mercy on me."

She began to tremble, afraid that she had overstepped her boundaries. She was conscious of the fact that her request to him for freedom and the groan of a dying slave would be given the same treatment—both ignored. She believed that her request for freedom would not be given any serious thought due to the strength of the rum, recognizing he was drunk by his slurred words, swaying uncontrollably and unsteady on his feet. *Nonetheless, I hope that my plea will find an opening in his heart and that he might remember it when not drunk.*

Mapp moved farther into the hut until he was towering over her. Penda stood rigid as he tried to regain his balance.

"Do you know what it means to be free?" Mapp asked her.

"Yes, suh," she said, weakly thinking of freedom in Lunda village.

"Free to do what? Sleep, eat monkeys, and dance? You are all lazy!" he shouted.

As if on cue, the big drum started beating, and as if out of breath, he said, "You are free! Why don't you say something?" he shouted as he stumbled forward.

Penda felt trapped, unable to put a voice to her feelings, unable to move.

He then made a choking sound like someone gasping. "Free all the slaves? That would be the end of me and this plantation."

"Free me," she said quietly.

His face and body began to tighten the way a turtle does pulling his head inside its shell.

"You are a handsome girl, you are comfortable here in your own hut, and I promise that I will free you one day but not yet. Unfortunately, I cannot run the plantation without slaves, but when the time comes, I'll let you go."

"When time be, suh?" she asked him.

"I cannot set you free and expect you to know how to take care of yourself. Where would you go? With the runaways?"

She knew he was not being honest and regretted being forced to converse with him. She knew she was caught in a trap with a promise to be freed. She had heard tales in her village growing up about a trapped hawk and a raccoon chewing their legs off to be free.

"What can I give to be free?" she let the question hang.

Mapp is right. If I am freed, what could I do and where would I go?

Penda did her best to conceal the fear his words had given her and to concentrate on the conversation but seemed like a cloud had enveloped her.

As Mapp continued to stand over her, she felt a mixture of emotions; feelings of anger, fear, hopelessness, and helplessness toward this man looking down on her. She hated him yet she did not want to hate him. Her father would say forgiveness is a mark of strength and he who walks in unforgiveness carries a destructive thunderstorm on his inside.

"When me no want to be free?" she asked him.

"The answer is no. I have changed my mind. You are a slave and will always be a slave."

That last statement stung even though she did not comprehend its full meaning. It was the tone with which the words were spoken and the look that accompanied it. She shut her eyes for a while and then opened them again, hoping to erase all that had been said.

She gingerly raised her head and looked him in the eye knowing that it was the first and most likely the last time she would take that chance.

Penda knew that as a slave, she was not permitted to look any master or mistress in the face.

He finally picked up his lantern and backed away out of the hut. She watched him stumbling down the path toward the common area. Penda remained fixed on the spot, listening as the cracking of the whip and his staggering grew faint, a sign that he was a distance away from the huts.

Sure, that Master was gone. Penda lay down and tried with difficulty to fall back asleep.

When she awoke, it was still dark, but she could see signs of the approaching dawn. Feeling restless, she got dressed and went outside. The air was brisk, and the morning still as she walked down the narrow path leading to the sea. For a moment, she considered running away as her last conversation with Mapp played in her head over and over. However, common sense prevailed, and turning around, she walked back toward the plantation.

The encounter she had with Mapp in the night brought to memory something she had witnessed between a cat and a mouse. After the first capture, the cat pretended to let the mouse go. He would pull his claw back far enough to give the mouse a false hope of escaping. The mouse sensing freedom would make a run for it, only to be caught by a fast paw, and a quick bite to its neck, trapping the mouse once again into the game. Penda watched this cat and mouse game for a while until the cat got careless and the mouse dashed off again this time to freedom but damaged and easy game for the next predator. Still, it had gotten away. She would never lose hope because it was said of her clan that they were like a lizard, if it lost its tail, it grew another. In the fight between the rock and the river, the river wins not because it is stronger but because of its persistence in flowing.

What Master Mapp was telling her, she was already aware of. She was learning how to survive by forcing herself to learn the language of the planters. They ate what was edible namely yams, beans, and sweet potatoes.

The following night, as Odon walked Penda to her hut, she asked him if he thought Massuh would sell them. "Yes, he can sell us if we don't please him, or if we get sick and can't work, or we get too old or something bad happens in the sugarcane field and we lose hand or foot wid machine. If Mapp gambles and lose, den he can't pay debt, or he have family that die or have wedding like we have in village and need money den he would sell we."

While Penda waited in the kitchen for her first day of work as a personal slave to the mistress, she passed the time talking to Gertrude the Cook and a little boy in the kitchen. The boy did not look as if he was five years old; she was sure of that.

"How old children be for de field?" she asked the cook.

"How old child be no matter to Massuh, dey go to de field any age."

The children she saw working alongside her during her first week in the field appeared to be younger than the boy. While

Gertrude rambled on about the Mapps and their drinking habits, Penda turned her attention to the little serious child who was hiding in the corner, and she thought of her brother when he was born and how close they became. His name was Nmadi, meaning *my father still lives*.

"Won't surprise me if Mistress kill she self wid pot liquor," Gertrude said, rousing the girl from her reverie.

"She won't," Penda countered, "'cause dat is de water left from boiled greens. Can't kill nobody."

"I know Mistress drinking water but not from sweet potato leaf," Gertrude answered, dropping the topic as the girl seemed not interested in conversing with her.

Having no response to the last statement, Penda turned away from the child. Gertrude looked about her mother's age, and in her village, a young woman Penda's age would not have had that conversation with a grown-up.

Penda picked up the boy and tickled him until his serious face melted into laughter.

There were times she held him on her lap and told him of Lunda village, the hills, and rivers as much as she could remember in a dialect unfamiliar to him. Her voice got softer and softer until she just mused quietly. What filled her mind in that state were scenes from the past: The night before she got captured, the slave auction, Kuba and Odon, and how they were settling in. She even remembered her father and mother, the village.

The quietness was broken by the boy wiggling on her lap indicating he wanted to go back to playing with his stones. As thoughts of her parents intruded, Penda closed her eyes to prevent the tears escaping, and to allow her mind to remain at home in Lunda village. She longed for her mother, or someone to talk to about those things that mothers talk to daughters about. She felt alone on the plantation and being in a hut by herself intensified the feeling of loneliness.

Every Monday was clothes washing day, and Mistress visited the kitchen. On that day, the week's allotment of groceries for the kitchen was delivered by the senior house staff.

"Dat woman don't know salt from sugar Gertrude chuckled under her breath, but she pretends to oversee the kitchen. Every Monday she goes through the cupboards looking for what she thinks may be hidden there."

Gertrude was the mistress of the kitchen, and everyone on the plantation knew it. She was brought from another plantation not strict in the use of Bible names.

While Gertrude and Penda were preparing the clothes and laundry for washing one Monday, she said, "Mistress Catherine marry Master Matthew because he family rich."

Penda remained quiet, not wanting to talk about Mistress. Gertrude continued to talk while Penda maintained a vacant look on her face, not wanting to engage in the conversation. Gertrude noticing, changed the subject to the task of laundry.

Penda's first day working in the big house started at noon. As Mistress Mapp's personal maid, Penda knew she was her attendant until whatever time her duties for her were done. As the enslaving mistress, she decided where, and when Penda worked and what food she ate, the girl could be punished when and how Mistress pleased. No two days could be the same. The length of her working day would change depending on the attitude of Mistress. Penda's daily duties began at noon and included carrying buckets of water up the stairs to fill the bathtub. When she got through bathing, she drained the tub and carried the water down. She would rub her skin after breakfast until she was satisfied, ironed clothes, and laid them out daily and would be at her beck and call until sometimes midnight. At the end of each day, though exhausted, Penda was happy she was not working in the field.

She went to Mistress's room by the back stairs, the way slaves entered.

"Open the shutters, not the one on the left, just the middle one," she barked.

Mistress knew that even if the girl stood on tiptoe, she would be too short to reach the upper shutters. She would have to use a chair but that was out of the question. She would never give permission for Penda to stand on her upholstered chairs. Penda became nervous when Mistress did not move but kept staring.

While Penda hesitated over what action to take, Mistress said, "Stupid, lazy girl," and left the room. Quickly she climbed onto the chair, pulled open the window, and opened the shutters. As she got down, something moved in front of her, and she froze. The movement stopped. It was her reflection in the wall mirror. She stood for a long time staring at the anxious, gaunt face with hollow cheeks, an emaciated body with spindly arms, that looked back at her. She stared for a while, then moved away.

After working in the big house for about two years, Penda noticed the structure of Mapp's house was not wood. The slave huts were little and made from wood with intertwined banana leaves for roofs, while Mistress had a tin roof. There was a library and a kitchen. It had five rooms, wood chairs, and a big wood table; there were windows with cloth covering them, which Mammy called curtains.

Another day, while Penda was working in the kitchen with Gertrude, the conversation turned to Kuba. She said, "You know Bassa just like Kuba when I come to Coconut Palms. He is tall and strong, and he fight all time wid overseer. He runs away many times and every time dey catch him and whip him. Last time he run away when dey catch him instead of cutting off he two legs as the slave law say, dey break dem. The bones then never heal dats why he rock side to side when he walk."

Penda had no response for the cook, so she turned her to thoughts of her brother. She would have liked to engage in a conversation with her, but as far as Penda was concerned, that was all before her time.

"He been a slave for fifty years, Gertrude continued, but forty he a field slave, then overseer. Nobody like him. He is now old, no hair on he head. He had many children, but Massuh sell dem to plantation in the center of de island to a Master Worrell at Sturges in Saint Thomas."

That night, Penda met Kuba at their secret place. They made sure no one was around to hear them speaking their dialect.

"Penda, I shame I can't free you. I have to run away from here, or I die." She heard the catch in his voice as he spoke.

"I don't want to be here alone. Odon is Master Mapp personal houseboy, and you in sugarcane field all day. Knowing you somewhere around help take away de loneliness."

"But me thought," said Kuba after he had listened to her, "remember Mapp say he could sell we any time to another plantation?"

"Yes, he said that, but I don't want to be alone," Penda whispered while her eyes sought anxiously for his facial expression in the dark.

"I know you feel lonely," he said. "But how me keep you safe here?" he asked her in a pleading voice.

"Then let we run away together we plant food like we do in Lunda." But even as she said it, she knew her conviction was as false as the illusion of her freedom. Then she pleaded with one of their gods Almaquah for help; the same god who had failed to protect them from their captors.

"Help me, help me!" She cried, covering her face with shaky hands uncertain of who her cries were really meant for.

Thinking of their experience on the ship, the uncertainty of their lives while reliving the fear and terror of standing naked while straw-colored men poked and prodded. The loss of family, a future, and a home was crippling. She became breathless and, for a moment, was aware of her heart pounding against her ribs. She became disoriented, and for what seemed like hours, she struggled to remember where she was.

The ship, its stench, fear and terror, the abuse of women and children, the hunger and the dying remained fresh in her memory for a long time. She would awake in the night after terrifying dreams of her raid and capture.

Kuba turned, and for a moment his face took on a look she did not recognize. All the times that they had met in their secret place, he was smiling. Tonight, in the moonlight, he seemed engaged in a wrestling match with something within himself.

"Penda," he finally said, then he stopped.

When she looked closer, she saw anguish clearly written on his face, probably mirroring the anguish written on her face.

Thoughts of running away accompanied her daily, but she rejected the thoughts as quickly as they came. Memories and images of whippings she had witnessed, quelled the thoughts along with her ignorance of the route to the runaway camp. Penda knew since she learned to count, she would count quietly if she witnessed a whipping, and each time those slaves very often received more lashes than the number prescribed in the laws. No one looked at the laws hanging in Mapp's library, as not many of the slaves could read. The thought of what could happen if she was caught brought a feeling of dread that paralyzed her ability to think rationally or initiate escape. *Where could I go where they won't find me? Was a question* left unanswered.

She thought of an experience she had with a mouse that had been caught by a cat. *We are all like the mouse*, she thought, *toyed with by Mapp and his overseers before they destroyed us. Like the mouse, we are not able to negotiate our freedom with our captors. Would we ever get an opportunity to be free?*

Each Sunday after church, the slaves gathered in a common area surrounded by huts. It was the one day that the overseers did not bother the slaves. Penda went for a stroll away from the area. Part of her was hoping to meet Kuba somewhere out there as he had been gone from Coconut Palms for several sugarcane harvests. It was not uncommon for him to jump out from behind a bush or tree and scare her. Sunday was the only day that the slaves did not go to the fields, nor did Penda have to be in the kitchen at dawn.

The sky was unusually blue with wisps of angel hair clouds. She noticed how freely the butterflies flitted about. Their freedom caused a yearning on the inside of her that she couldn't explain. Men laughed and talked among themselves like the elders did in her village. They were squatting on the ground chatting, eating, and singing as she walked to the edge of the huts taking time to look at the different plants. She took note of the large tamarind tree by the pond loaded with tamarinds as well as the hibiscus and the bougainvillea. Passing the sugar apple and soursop trees the girl noticed for the first time all the leaves on the banana trees were open in an arch. On some of the plants, she saw a purple tip of a bud pushing its way up to the sun.

At the foot of the banana tree, Penda's eye followed a procession of black ants going in and coming out of a small tunnel in the earth. The ants going in were carrying what looked like tiny half circles while those leaving were obviously in a hurry. Leaving them, she kept walking and within a short time she stepped into a quiet and beautiful area. She could not believe that such a beautiful area existed on the plantation. Entranced with such beauty, she walked further into the trees without looking back, then she panicked on realizing the singing of the slaves had grown increasingly faint. She continued walking as her heartbeat quickened, afraid of being thought of as trying to run away. The last person she prayed not to meet was Bassa the Overseer who may have thought that she was going to join the runaway camp. She sat down on a tree stump to rehearse the conversation of her last meeting with Odon and his plan to steal gunpowder for the runaways to use in their planned revolt.

Her heartbeat quickened, afraid of being discovered, yet she planned to make this newly discovered and secluded spot her place. She would tell Kuba about it the next time they met, and she would make a shrine to their gods. Penda made a mental list of the prayers she would send out to their gods, the moon, thunder, the morning star, the crops, the rain, and the gods of their ancestors. She became excited at her plans and the discovery of such a peaceful place. She found a piece of charcoal with which she made a mark on a tree at the edge of the path, her intention being to go there every Sunday when the slaves rested or worked their gardens.

Then she saw something that would forever change her life. She saw him, the red shirt and short pants, the dusty feet they belonged to Odon no mistake. Her brain slowed and refused vehemently every attempt to comprehend what she saw. Then suddenly she was flooded with panic and the full realization of what she had just seen. Yes, she recognized him by the red shirt and short black trousers that were the uniform of Master's personal slaves. The shirt was opened exposing his chest, while his face and body were badly bruised and covered in blood, but there was still something about the body that she recognized as Odon's.

Something about the feet that were black and not mud. She could see marks left by the hot pincers on both sides of his chest and the rivulets of dry blood that had flowed out of the wounds. The faint odor of roasted flesh still lingered though ever so faint. The image hit her like a lightning bolt, she shut her eyes, but she had already seen it. Fear rose and spread over her body, making her hands sweaty and trembling. She grasped her throat first, then her hands ripped at the neck of the oversized dress she was wearing. She remembered stumbling backward gasping, then falling over something and hitting the ground hard.

Tears rolled down Penda's face hot and fast, as she heaved herself off the ground trembling and afraid but not wanting to draw any attention to the scene. Her heart was loud in her ears. She ran stumbling trying to fight her way back into consciousness. She never thought she would see him burnt with hot pincers or his body stretched unrecognizable from being on the rack. Then she heard screams.

Maybe they know, she thought, *maybe the others have seen it too.*

As her hand moved involuntarily to her mouth, Penda realized that the voice she heard had come from her, before her world went black. When she awoke, she was on the floor of old Mammy's hut. Mammy was like a mother to all the slaves being one of the oldest women on the plantation.

"I must be dreaming," Penda repeated as she tried to understand what she had just seen.

"Why, Lord? Why!" Mammy shouted when Penda had recovered enough from the shock and was able to relate what she had seen.

"O God, in heaven," Mammy prayed, "have mercy on us. Our lives are surrounded by so much that be evil. My heart feel grief over Odon's death. Who be so wicked, Lawd? He dead, but you live forever you rule and reign no matter what happens on this plantation. Have mercy Lord as the master and overseers show their power over us doing such wicked and brutish things. Lord, I humbly ask you to loose these chains from us and make we free. De Bible dat I read say in de book of James dat you don't choose one human over the other cause you make all of us. The masters can't take a breath unless you give it to them. Right now, Lord, it look like you show favor to them who do we wrong cause they prosper while we are dying. Help, Lord, because you are a just God that rights wrongs, dis Bible tell me so."

Penda fought to keep her eyes closed so she could keep her mind on the prayer and her thoughts from wandering to the images of Odon's body at the foot of a tree. Tears squeezed from the corners of her eyes, while her mouth opened and closed without forming words.

Mammy continued, "God, you see all things. Bring conviction to de heart of who do dis deed. Help us not to be afraid as your word command cause you say you didn't give we a spirit of fear. We look to you today for de time when all dis end in Jesus's name. Amen."

As the prayer ended abruptly, Mammy's tears flowed as she voiced memories of all her children who had been torn from her breast and sold. Finally, she gave way to the sorrow she was feeling and the grief.

Mammy brought Penda some herb tea as she laid on the floor. After a long time, Penda was able to pour out her heart to Mammy in what sounded like an incoherent rambling noise.

The following morning, as dawn was approaching, Penda awoke with a start as images of the horror of the previous day returned. She remembered every detail of the discovery. Her eyes filled with tears that ran unchecked on the mud floor. Then she thought it was a bad dream. The words of her last conversation with Odon played over and over in the girl's mind. Just a few days ago, he had confided in her the plan to join Kuba at the runaway camp.

"I'll run away with Kuba after I steal this last shipment of gunpowder." Penda noticed how well he spoke as she studied his plan for a few minutes. Something about it did not suit Penda.

"How are you going to do this, and what happen if Bassa catches you?" she asked him.

"Me don't know, but if me stay here, me die," he answered in a dejected tone.

He seemed to be resolute in his plan to join the runaways. His English vocabulary was markedly improved as he learned words and numbers by helping Master balance his books.

Feelings of guilt flooded Penda's heart. She tried to get up from the floor, but her legs became weak causing her to buckle at the knees. The air was suffocating as she tried to get up again, but her legs seemed unable to give her any support. Frustrated with her efforts, Penda remained sitting on the ground. She bowed her head, closed her eyes, clenched her jaws, and pressed her mouth tightly against her knees to keep from whaling.

One question she rehearsed over and over was, *Who did this and why?*

Guilt filled the girl's heart because she felt some responsibility for his death although she did not know what could have been done to stop it. How could she have been so stupid to believe that Odon could get away with a plan so dangerous and a risk to his life?

Maybe I should have been the one to be burned, she thought. "Lord, be merciful, forgive me." She wailed. She imagined how Odon must have screamed as the hot pincers were put to his body or how he must have pleaded with his killer to spare his life.

"I should have done something," she spoke aloud, "I should have warned him about the dangers of following Kuba and his crazy plans."

No questions were asked about Odon's death. It was announced at roll call the next day that his burial would be at sundown. It was common for slaves to be buried quickly. She couldn't share her grief; she could only bear it in silence.

"Oh, Odon," she moaned.

At the funeral, Mapp said, "Philemon was a good house servant. He worked hard, learned to read the accounts quickly, and was good with them. He was loved by all the house and field slaves, and they are here to say farewell."

The slaves left one by one, leaving Penda alone, staring at the heaped earth. Four years of memories were replayed over and over like Odon walking her home after midnight when her duties were done or the first time he stole gunpowder and almost got caught. The only time she could pause his final image from her mind was when she was busy. She could only think of Odon, the sight of his foot and his lifeless body, already cold sitting at the foot of a tree.

"Food is scarce at the camp, Penda. We have more people than we have food. Maybe in another full moon, we will be able to get some goods. The drums at Christ Church say that the governor is on his way to see Mapp, and they say he will be here tomorrow, spending a few days talking to plantation owners and spying on things. He will bring gunpowder and bullets as he did last visit. Tell Oden we need both and tell him to take everything he can manage and hide it behind the big cactus tree."

Penda shook her head. "He did that three months ago when the governor was here, and you remember he nearly got caught. He had a bag full of gunpowder." Samson the Guard was looking for him at the same time because Mapp needed attention. He hid in the cave while Samson searched for him. Samson was just about to enter the cave when as if in obedience to a command the tide came in with full force. The tide kept Samson out, but the guns and gunpowder got soaked.

"I think you should leave Odon out of it this time."

"My mission is to free as many slaves as I can," Kuba said with a determined look.

On the first request to get gunpowder, Odon turned Kuba down, but he was not deterred.

"Why can't you do it?" Kuba asked him.

"Because I remember last time."

After much questioning by Kuba, Penda could see that Odon's defenses were beginning to waver. Despite their deep friendship, Odon was afraid of two things, being caught and betraying Mapp's trust in him. These things he had revealed to Penda. Finally, as a compromise, Odon shouted "This will be de last time me do dis for you, and I hope me gods and me ancestors help. If dey do, it be de biggest haul."

"Don't worry about nothing. It is my job to take care of you at the camp," Kuba assured Odon.

On hearing those words, Odon looked relieved, and he gave in, promising to steal the guns and gunpowder.

The time for the yearly planters meeting in Bridgetown had arrived. Mr. Mapp left early on Monday morning, and Catherine

Mapp left Monday afternoon to visit her friend at Sturge's plantation in Saint Thomas. With the house empty of the Mapp, everyone and everything, including the furniture, seemed to breathe a sigh of relief. Odon decided that the three of them would sleep in the master's bed while he was away. Before sleeping, they would taste the same rum that Master Mapp drank every night.

Odon filled his glass to overflowing, and Penda filled her glass also. She took two big gulps before the pungency made her cough and splutter. She thought it disgusting. Kuba's face showed fear as she continued to cough uncontrollably. Then Penda took another gulp of the rum saying that her throat felt warm. That gulp was followed by another gulp, and then another until the counting stopped. Kuba was talking, Penda opened her mouth to ask a question but didn't finish. She got on the bed, it was cold and soft, and she could feel sleep creeping over her body along with a fear of being caught.

"Master won't like we in his bed," Kuba said.

"We don't care dey all gone so we sleep here," Odon answered.

When Penda closed her eyes, she felt as if she was flying in a circle up to the ceiling. Then she would open her eyes and be on the bed.

"Dis what de rum do to you?" she asked them.

They must have fallen asleep because Penda was jerked awake by a lot of shouting. For a minute, she felt disoriented and confused. It had been a strange feeling but a good one sleeping in a real bed after all the years on the floor. She tried to quickly orient herself to her whereabouts as she recognized Master Mapp as the one shouting.

The evening sun was streaming through the slightly ajar shutters, and her eyes made a quick sweep of the room hoping to find landmarks that would hasten her orientation. She saw the clock and chest of drawers, Mapp's bed, and Odon lying next to her. She opened her mouth to call out for Odon, but her mouth felt dry as chalk and Kuba was nowhere to be seen in the room.

"Odon," she croaked, but her voice came out sounding gruff.

Odon woke up, then he heard the shouting. They leaped out of bed and scrambled under it, just as Mapp flung the door open, still shouting, and slammed the bedroom door shut behind him. Odon and Penda looked at each other, lying as still as two corpses.

Mapp's boots could be seen moving from side to side, dropping mud as he walked back and forth across the room. Then he kicked off his boots. Most of the time, Mapp was mumbling incoherently, while at other times, he was cursing and damning. Suddenly, Mapp stopped his pacing and paused head tilted as if listening. Penda was too afraid to move her head to look at Odon. She watched Mapp pull a chair over to the window and sit down directly across from where they were lying. They were now trapped in a confined place under the bed.

Penda began to fret silently, asking how long they would have to stay hidden. She could see the evening shadows through the plantation shutters moving slowly across the floor in their direction.

Mapp's breathing was heavy at times, but on others, his respiration was interrupted by sighs, while at other times, his breath came fast and shallow as if he was being chased.

A lizard ran over their faces, as Mapp moved his right foot, then he crossed one leg over the other, then he separated them and walked across the floor again. The lizard returned and scrambled back in the other direction over them again. Mapp remained sitting, and he stayed there. Penda began to twist and turn, needing to breathe air that was not laden with stale rum breathed out by Odon in her face. She also needed moisture for her dry mouth, but Odon put a hand on her shoulder with firm pressure reminding her to remain still and quiet.

As their eyes met in the darkness under the bed, a silent question was asked, "Are we going to get out of this place?"

Mapp began to mumble again, pushing the chair back and pacing as before. Suddenly he fell to the floor an arm's length from where Odon was lying. His eyes were open and fixed on them staring as if he could see where they were hiding. Blood was running from his mouth onto the floor. Before they could run, someone was in the doorway. Penda knew she was trapped with a full bladder and overwhelmed with fear of the outcome. It was Dorothy, the second cook, in the doorway.

Seeing Master Mapp lying on the floor, Dorothy called his name out loud, probably believing he was drunk. Bassa the Overseer came in on the heels of Dorothy, got down on the floor, and turned Master's body over putting an ear to his chest.

On seeing the blood running from his nose, the cook's legs went limp, and she staggered across the room, shouting for one of the drivers to go get the doctor. The one doctor for the surrounding plantations took hours to come when called. Penda and Odon knew it would take a long time as there was only one doctor for Coconut Palms and the surrounding plantations.

Penda's head started to throw out one lie after another that she would tell if caught but each one was assessed and discarded for the other. At times, she carried on a conversation with her imaginary Mammy.

"There's no excuse for lying." She heard Mammy say.

"But, Mammy, Master Mapp tell we lies," she often replied. Then Mammy would say, "Penda, Bible say God hates lies, and it is difficult to fight a lie or hide from it. A person can shield themself from de blows of a whip or a slap, but dere is no way to get away or ward off the blows of a lying tongue. De life of a person can be put in danger by lying lips. Many people on dis plantation me see whipped or killed over a lie."

"Why should we get whipped for stealing or lying, Mammy? They tell us don't steal, but dey steal we mothers and fathers, all we family."

"Well, what dey say and what dey do far apart."

"Was it wrong to tell Mistress Catherine that I liked my name, Sarah? I lied cause I afraid what she would do."

"Penda, pressure to not do the right thing will come every day. It may come in the big house or from you when lonely or from Kuba. The right thing is to tell the truth no matter what."

Unable to argue any further with Mammy, Penda concluded that if they got caught, if given a choice she would ask to be whipped, the most common form of punishment.

Her thoughts moved to Kuba. She worried that he may have been caught. She knew how he longed to be free from the harsh treatments that were meted out by the slave owners and overseers. She thought of their secret meeting place next to the gully where the bushy vines had formed an enclosure, providing a perfect hiding spot.

She thought of their last Sunday together and his long periods of silence as if preoccupied. When he started to talk, he blurted out, "Drums say Emode and Ezekiel from another plantation marry. You and me now on plantation two sugarcane harvests and no jump de broom."

"What you say?" Penda asked, not sure she heard correctly. He repeated his last statement.

"Why you look at we life to Emode and Ezekiel? He much her age. Master wants a lot of babies but me no want marry old man."

"Yes, I dream of jumping broom and children, but me see enough on plantation to know dat not possible."

"I can't believe Emode is married. She not older dan me. Now me can't be friend wid she on Sundays because she is a married woman."

"You right, nothing we can do," he said as she watched him getting angry.

"Always something we can do. Never say never. In de village, me watch many times de ant tries to reach de food that is sacrificed to the gods, but it is in de fold of a wrapped leaf. Nothing is easy."

She watched him wince, but it was too late to change her words. *What is the use of quarreling?* she asked herself. She decided she couldn't do anything about his thoughts, but she would own hers. It was wrong for her to lose her patience and she was sorry for her sharp words.

"Kuba, me sorry." Penda thought she knew him since they grew up together, but since they had been on the plantation, she was not sure any longer. Her thoughts did not match his. Something more than their village, upbringing, or culture was separating them.

"Me won't always be a slave, and me won't have children me can't watch grow to be man," he said forcefully as he turned and walked away.

Fear for Kuba returned, her hands became sweaty as she pictured everything that could happen.

Penda was jolted back to her surroundings by the voice of the overseer repeating to the cook that Mapp was dead.

"Look at de man, he ain't breathing," a statement he kept repeating.

Cook finally left the room, convinced that Master Mapp was gone. Bassa stood up, then knelt again.

Maybe Penda or Odon gulped and swallowed hard, or Bassa sensed someone other than him was in the room. He glanced under the bed. When he looked, his eyes met Odon's staring back at him.

"Out!" he shouted, as he grabbed Odon and dragged him from under the bed. Odon had gained size living in the big house where food was plentiful.

Penda remained under the bed, hidden from Bassa's view. Odon punched him hard in the face, the girl watched in fear as Basso wilted, and went limp. Odon hit him again and this time Bassa dropped to the floor as his whip fell from his hand. Penda ran out from under the bed climbing over the bodies of Mapp and Bassa.

They bolted through the door in shock, but Odon remembered to shut and lock the door.

"Let Bassa explain how he come to be in a room with a dead man." They ran to a nearby field of tall grass to get their stories together and to allow Odon to recover from the experience. There they both waited and for what seemed like a long time said nothing. Finally, a decision was made that Odon would go to the big house as normal for his evening duties, and Penda would go to Hagar, tribal name Gwendoya.

Odon loved Penda but was afraid to tell her in case she told Kuba. He had overheard Mapp making plans to marry her to Ebenezer a slave from Sturges plantation in Saint Thomas. Images of them being sold and Penda married for breeding filled him with a fear he could not explain. Every night when he lay on his palette, he wished she was in the hut with him.

"I can't stay here," he said bitterly, "I know you love Kuba. Don't want to spend any more years on this plantation, hoping for freedom. I don't want to lose any more years, hoping and waiting for an end." He looked like he wanted to say more while she didn't trust herself to advise him.

Penda stared at him, her tired body and brain only half understanding. She studied him. So she allowed him to speak to her about those things that made him despair or threw him in anguish.

While he talked, Penda was trying to forget what had just happened, but now lying in the grass, thinking of what could happen to them, brought a wave of fear for what could happen to them over an impulsive act. They lay there for a moment until they were able to pull themselves and their stories together, and then they stood up and walked toward Gwen's hut, believing she was still working in the field. Gwendoya (Hagar) was a big, tall woman with big arms. She looked as if her head rested on her shoulders. She was taller than all the men on the plantation and could head more sugarcane than everyone in her group. Bassa never bothered her. No one seemed to know where she came from. The story around the huts had it that she had one daughter who was sold at birth, and she never had another child.

Kuba was anxiously waiting for them. A decision was made unanimously that Penda and Kuba would run away that night, and Odon, as a pretense, would go to the big house to see if Mapp had returned and required his service.

"Why did you leave me and Odon in Mapp's bed? We afraid something happen to you," Penda asked Kuba.

"While you pass out from de rum, me search Mapp house for guns and gun powder."

"You and Odon foolish and me want no part in that foolishness. One morning, after we talk about Emode and Ezekiel wedding me look for Preacher Brown going to de sea. Drums say he go early to bathe every morning."

*****

Odon hurried up the stairs to Mapp's room, finding the door locked from the outside with the key jutting out of the keyhole just as he left it. On opening the door, he found Bassa sitting on the floor next to Mapp's body, unable to say what happened or how he came to be there. As Odon left, promising him he would get help, he saw the cook approaching the doctor.

They felt safe knowing that Bassa could not remember any of the details leading up to Mapp's lifeless body being found on the floor.

The doctor concluded that Mapp suffered a severe heart attack and a broken neck, which he thought may have been from excessive rum consumption.

"What happen to we if map dead?" Penda asked Kuba who just shook his head without audible response.

What would happen to Odon? Fear gripped her as in her mind she had images of the three of them being sold to different plantations.

Penda was unable to forget the startled look on Mapp's face as he lay on the floor, the sound of the thud as he fell, she relived the sound of his heavy footsteps as he paced the floor, and the emotion when they were discovered under the bed. There was pounding in her ears and sweat poured down her body as she anticipated the journey planned for later that night. Penda related the incident to Kuba many times while they waited for nightfall along with many questions asked about the runaway camp. Anxiously Penda went to the doorway of Hagar's hut many times to check on the depth of darkness. Unknown to them, a man stood behind the mango tree, waiting to follow them for the reward.

Kuba decided he and Penda would run before the slaves returned from the fields. "'Cause in de field overseer busy," Kuba added as an afterthought. Kuba divided up his haul from the big house into two sacks.

"I carry de big one," he told her.

Kuba placed the lighter sack on Penda's head. It gave her such a strange eerie feeling she said to him, "Carrying gunpowder on my head don't feel right. Me not used to carrying dese heavy things."

She had never carried sugarcane on her head. It wasn't the weight Penda concluded but the technique she didn't have. Watching the men and women carry the bundles of cane so effortlessly made her think she could do it. She had never learned the technique but observed the apparent ease with which the long sugarcane was balanced.

Carrying so much weight on her head she thought it was doable if the journey was short and the land ahead was flat. It was none of these. She knew even though she had never gone to the runaway camp she wouldn't be able to make it. From Kuba, she learned the camp was far away, but she would try for him. So putting one foot in front of the other, Penda followed Kuba. It was a slow-moving torture full of sweat and mosquitoes, and of stumbling every couple steps. Holding the sack on her head with both hands reduced Penda's ability to avoid the approach of face-level branches that slapped her face, while Kuba was barely stooped under his load she observed from behind him.

"Just put it down," Kuba kept saying. "I know it's heavy."

But whatever her reason, the more he said it, the more stubborn and obsessed she became with making it to the camp before nightfall.

"I can do it," she kept telling Kuba.

But to continue trying, she had to go at an even slower pace than before, forcing him to wait for her to catch up at times. Without any landmarks or signs, Penda feared they were going in circles. It seemed like Kuba had forgotten the road to the runaway camp. There was nothing to give them clues as to where the path was leading. They wandered for a while until they heard a muffled cough coming from behind them sending a chill down Penda's spine.

She prayed, asking Mammy's God or one of her gods, to not let them be captured. "Lead us to freedom, Lord," she prayed, believing that one of them would answer.

Kuba motioned for her to keep following him without talking, and she was compliant though her body ached more from fear than tiredness. She trailed behind him dragging her feet that had become very tired.

The sun was sinking lower and lower, and shadows were dwindling, yet they kept, walking and seeking a place to rest before her shadow left, believing her village saying that if a person's shadow abandons them, they will die.

They finally saw an opening near a cliff and entered. It was a dark place where they were greeted by an unexpected host of mosquitoes that attacked them mercilessly.

With difficulty, Penda reached up to remove the sack from her head, surprised to find a space where she could sit. There was no human smell, so they crawled a little further in until Kuba judged that they were far enough away from the entrance. Feeling faint from hunger and exhaustion they wanted to rest a while before continuing. But after the rest, Penda decided she did not want to continue the journey, thinking it was a foolish endeavor, and she felt close to collapse.

What exactly was the point? she asked herself as she engaged in a self-debate asking herself questions. *Should I continue to the camp- will I even make it? Or should I go back to the plantation and take my punishment?*

They sat silent and pensive. With a heavy heart, she thought of her parents, sisters, and brother. Some of her thoughts were spent on Kuba who she sensed wanted freedom. He had shared on many occasions his fear of being captured and his plan for if it ever happened. He had told her he would rather die than be captured again. She sensed at that moment that Kuba may have been afraid as he wasn't forthcoming with any further instructions or plans for the night. A couple of years had passed on the plantation where they witnessed cruel treatments that may have scarred them both, yet he seemed more focused on the load than on her.

Things that she had stopped thinking about began to surface, the mountains, family, the sounds of the village with its night sounds, and freedom. After a while, the girl sensed a feeling of tiredness stealing over them. Penda felt around in the dark for a comfortable spot, and then she lay down, positioning herself to avoid the roots and stones that protruded from the ground. However, the effort was futile as neither of them could find a comfortable position to sleep. To calm herself, Penda whispered a passage from the Bible in Isaiah about the Lord being with her always. They rested and Penda must have fallen asleep. It was well past dawn, but still dark when she woke up tired and hungry. She had obviously slept, but Kuba was gone.

She decided to be back at the big house before Mistress returned. She got herself together to leave as she mentally reviewed her last conversation with Kuba and how angry he seemed.

Outside the cave, Penda heard footsteps. She stooped and backed to the end of the enclosure as a man's profile filled the opening. All she could see was his torso. Whoever it was seemed very tall. From the position of his hands, she could see he was carrying something.

"Where you be?" A man's voice Penda did not recognize asked.

She said nothing; fear closed and dried her throat.

"Me know you in dere." Penda was now sure it was Bassa. She hesitated to answer not knowing the man's plan.

"I walk wid you back to plantation. I be no bad man, I be father. I got five childen dat Mapp he sell. Me no want sell you. Come we go."

"I'm h-here," she finally stammered as she recognized the voice of the head overseer and moved toward the opening.

Penda felt relief at being found but it was mixed with sadness and fear. She wanted to know what happened to Mapp, so she said, "Me hear Mapp sick so me afraid mistress sell me to another plantation."

"He not sick, he dead. Doctor come yesterday, and he say he break his neck. Come, Mistress be back by noon today."

This was not what Penda expected such kindness from the man who seemed so stern when they met. Though the situation had gone from bad to worse in one night, she found some solace in the thought that maybe things were not as bad as they seemed.

CHAPTER 4

Preparations for burying Master Mapp's body began immediately once the doctor confirmed his death. The site chosen for his burial was away from the common area where Sunday services were conducted. The spot was directly across from the upstairs window of the big house, next to the grave of Mapp senior and enclosed by a wooden gate. His box was hastily made as two days was the maximum time a body could be held in the heat. For two days after his death, the slaves were allowed to stop work and prepare for his burial, a major event. No one in the fields grieved for him. They grieved for themselves and the mass sale of the plantation they anticipated would follow. Fear was visible on all the faces present. They knew that the death of the master often threatened the sale of the plantation, including the slaves.

The funeral was attended by Catherine Mapp, the slaves at Coconut Palms, and planters from nearby plantations.

After a couple of hymns, Preacher Brown spoke, "The Lord giveth and the Lord taketh away. Master Mapp died too young."

The attendees listened, and those who understood made moaning noises.

"I don't know if we should be happy or sad on this occasion. We are sorry to see him go at such a young age but glad he did not suffer. Death pulled Matthew out of life abruptly, but he is now in heaven and will never be sick or feel pain again. The people God puts in our lives are only for a season. We don't understand why, but we know that He knows all things, and one day, we will understand it better by and by."

Preacher Brown then admonished the people to not forget their master, the slaves, and the planters. He asked them to help Catherine as best as they could.

Everyone looking at Catherine believed she may have been drinking because of her unsteady gait and flushed face.

Rumors had begun to circulate even before Matthew's death that Catherine began drinking heavily after her last miscarriage. Some afternoons when Penda walked into the house Mistress would be totally disoriented in time, not knowing the day, month, or season.

When she walked to the front of the gathering, she looked as if she wanted to speak but being unable to do so, she closed her eyes and folded her hands tightly over her chest. Words of consolation were spoken by the planters from nearby plantations and their wives, after which Catherine turned and walked back to the big house.

That night, while Penda got Mistress ready for bed, she listened to her while she had a conversation with herself as if alone.

"Matthew's abrupt end is perplexing to me, and I do not know how I feel right now. All the money my husband made from sugar could not guarantee his life. He made a lot of money from the sugarcane, yet it could not buy him an extension of days from death. Matthew would walk away from having to witness a runaway slave being whipped. He just could not stomach the cruel and inhumane treatment that was meted out to them by the overseers. He had great difficulty ordering a man whipped or tortured because he believed that cruelty was ineffective at producing adherence to slave laws. His three greatest fears were losing slaves to death, a revolt, or being forced to sell the plantation and return to England broke.

"When Master William, my last baby died. I didn't think I could ever smile or laugh again. I felt God had smiled on me giving me a living son after four miscarriages. Then suddenly he was taken from me.

"Why did I agree to come here to Barbados? There was so much talk about unlimited money to be gained from sugar. The letter from Mathew's father summoning him to Barbados mentioned health problems. Matthew thought the health problem was referring to malaria fever, a common malady. But when we arrived, he was not suffering from malaria but syphilis in its end stage, and his mind destroyed. When Matthew first discussed emigrating, I considered letting him come first and when settled I would follow just like the planter's wife at Bagatelle had done. We had never set foot outside Lancashire England and paid no attention to the stories his father told on his visits. Matthew had started to vacillate on whether to remain on the island or sell the plantation and return home to England.

"Matthew and his father were like everyone who came to Barbados on the promise of becoming rich. It was not long before we were dealing with humidity, intense heat, and mosquitoes. Unfamiliar fruit made us ill, while unknown diseases like dysentery and African fevers made us weak. For some of the planters, this condition passed, but others died.

"No one told us the production of sugar was at the mercy of unforeseen circumstances like hurricanes, drought, plagues, rats, fluctuation in sugar prices, or bad health and death of slaves. Initially, I had no problem with the slaves being preached to on Sundays. Sometimes I became indignant as I listened to Brown spewing out twisted nonsense to people who could not read or write.

"I never set myself to learn about the slaves as people or basic human beings with needs like mine. Things like the improvisations they had to make to survive, or why we were doing what we did believing it made them conform, or why they seemed to have more capacity for suffering than us. When we removed their babies or their children and sold them, the women seemed to forget and recover as quickly as a dog, or a cow does when their babies are removed. What surprised me most was how quickly after a severe, near-fatal whipping, they were able to go back to the fields, and resume their daily lives."

At the end of Catherine's monologue, Penda understood enough English words to get the gist of it. Penda kept her head down as was the custom and nodded at pauses. What the girl understood was that Catherine had lost all reason to live. Since Mapp's death, Mistress had been drinking excessively every day.

Mapp's brother William and his wife arrived almost immediately after the funeral. They knew nothing about Mapp's death or about running a plantation. It was winter in England, and they thought of waiting out the winter months in tropical weather. Thankfully, the plantation was not sold as expected, and William became the new master. With the plantation settled, plans were made to escort Catherine back to England as her mental health was showing no signs of improving.

Penda's first impression of William was he was short like his brother, pale in skin with piercing blue eyes.

*****

It was weeks after the funeral Kuba came to their meeting place. There was slight bruising on his face.

"I ask Preacher Brown to marry we," he said.

"What?" Penda shouted.

"One morning, after we talked about Emode and Ezekiel jumping de broom, me tell drums me want to jump broom to make you wife."

"Who will marry we?" me drummed the question.

"Your Preacher Brown," the drums answered.

"Where me find him?" I asked the drums.

"He bathes at de sea every morning early as slaves go to field," drums answered me. "One morning, after some heavy rains and storms, I wait for Preacher. Me take path going to sea hoping to see preacher. I hide while he takes sea bath."

"It be a big chance I take, as he could tell Massuh."

"Morning, Suh, I want ask you to marry me and Sarah wid broom," me said, keeping me head down.

"Who are you?" Preacher Brown asked. "I don't know you. Are you new to the plantation?"

"No, suh, my name Kuba, and I want make Sarah wife."

"Don't know a Kuba," Preacher said. "Names are from the Bible."

He waited as if he wanted me to say more. He would not return this boy to Mapp's plantation if he was a runaway because his heart hurt for the slaves who could not be free. "God made all people free, but boys like this young man are enslaved for the money they bring to the planters."

"Why did you run away?" he asked.

Kuba kept quiet as he did not know many words like Preacher. He tried to speak very slowly, hoping he could understand him.

"Suh, in me village, man born free. On dis plantation, me see people dying so me run away to be free."

"Walk with me," Preacher mimed, and Kuba followed him to the tall sugarcane.

Preacher Brown had already formulated a plan that if seen by Mapp's men, he would pretend that he was returning him to the plantation.

They left the sea, walking the path where the sugarcane was tall enough to hide them. Kuba poured out his heart to Brown in limited words and mimes as at that moment his love for Penda overruled any fear or perceived plot the preacher may have had.

"Sarah cannot be married by me. The custom on this plantation is Mapp chooses the husband, and he reads the service from the gallery of the big house. Master has already arranged for Sarah to marry Israel from the plantation in Saint John," Brown said with finality.

It shouldn't have stung Kuba to learn this, but it did. *After all, she be property of Master* was his conclusion.

Kuba felt an ache in his chest. He could picture it he had seen enough marriages in his two years here.

Finally, after what seemed a long time, Preacher said, "Yes, I will marry you the next night Master and Mistress are away." This said he turned and walked toward the Big House.

In the face of Kuba, Preacher saw what he believed to be something genuine. The boy's motive for singling him out and asking remained a puzzle, yet he decided to grant his request aware that slaves were forced to marry against their will just to increase numbers for the planters through indiscriminate breeding. He had witnessed the broom jumping of Anna and Gershom.

Kuba's mouth opened and closed, but no sound came out. Then as if summing up courage, he said to Penda, "Me fraid of all straw-colored men and don't know if to trust Preacher Brown. He say yes, but—"

Penda and Kuba knew that Preacher would be breaking the law by marrying a runaway. "Don't want to die, or Master sell we," was Kuba's last response on the subject.

Penda knew that Brown had married many slaves. It was rumored that they were forced to do so against their will or choice but matched up by their plantation owners and overseers. No feelings of love were considered, it was just an arrangement, aimed at giving birth to babies to increase the workforce as soon as they were able. Kuba had witnessed the jumping of the broom with Adah and Gershom. Mapp had picked out Gershom and told him "You will marry Anna."

On the day of the wedding, Kuba and Penda arrived at the beach while it was still dark. The plantation seemed asleep when she left her hut. She wore her loose dress which she had washed the day before. Mammy twisted her hair and gave her some bright-colored beads to wear around her neck, and a wreath of yellow flowers she carefully picked and made for the occasion. She also gave her a shell saying "Dis is the last one. I am giving this to you believing you will leave dis plantation. I won't leave but I believe God that you will."

"This must be over, and I have to get back before I am missed," Penda whispered to Kuba, forgetting that the Mapps were away at a convention.

Preacher Brown asked Kuba, "Do you want this woman?" To Penda, he asked, "Do you want this boy?"

At weddings on the plantation, two people would hold the broom at both ends, and the couple would jump the broom. Since only Preacher was there, the broom was placed on the ground, and they held hands and jumped over it. Then Preacher after he read a verse from the Bible said to Kuba, "The Bible says man and woman leave and cleave. They become one and should not be sold or separated. You are now man and wife." Preacher left them promising to keep Bassa occupied should he encounter him. He wanted them to sleep together as man and wife that night consummating the marriage. As daybreak approached, Kuba held her vowing his love for her and promising never to leave her. Knowing that he could never keep that promise, he left for the camp with a heavy heart.

Brown was not unaware of the difficult position Kuba had placed him in. He had said yes to his request, though, he knew permission was granted by the slave owner who in this case would be Mapp.

*****

For weeks, there were rumors that Governor Goring was coming. Penda overheard the cook telling Matilda one of the washerwomen.

"He come not as friend only to order lot of beatings."

There was terror in her eyes as she spoke of mock trials and brutal punishments he introduced on his visits to the plantation.

"Every time he come, Mapp make a big banquet. We cook many foods many days."

A week later, a carriage brought the governor with two of his house servants, Nahum and Hosea. A meeting was planned for planters from the five surrounding plantations to attend. The meeting was centered around keeping slaves from running away and preventing the drums from sending messages. Six planters, including Mapp and their body servants, were present for the reading of the new laws to be introduced. Leftovers from the big meal were given to the slaves.

The following day, while walking into the big house to begin her duties, Penda heard men's voices coming from the verandah. The planters were already there awaiting the discussion of the slave laws. As she listened, she recognized Preacher Brown's voice and assumed the other voice was that of the Governor. She peeked around the verandah, saw the backs of two of the planters, and then saw Mapp and the other planters, but they were quiet.

"Brown your preaching to the slaves has not made a damned bloody difference," the governor said.

"Until the slaves are properly treated as human beings and given food, the dying will not stop," Preacher Brown responded with a hint of irritation. "Slaves whipped to death solves nothing. The first problem concerns language. Slaves are unable to understand the sermons. There is obviously a problem of communication. They are illiterate field slaves, Governor. They cannot read, write, or speak the language."

The governor looked at Preacher Brown and shrugged with a look of annoyance on his face. "You must have obedience from the slaves!" the governor shouted.

"Are you blaming the planters for the drought or the hurricanes that have ruined the crops? Is it our fault that the slaves we buy are lazy?" another voice asked.

Then Mapp spoke, "What can I do to keep my slaves from running away? Right now, the bush and caves are full of runaways. What is your answer, Governor?"

Then the governor's face became red as a beet, and he said, "Runaways from this plantation some years ago are causing great trouble for the planters on the island. Word has come to me that a revolt against all the planters on the island is being planned. I have written a new set of laws to send a warning to them and all the slaves who are thinking of joining. The leader of runaway slaves shall be pinched three times with hot iron and hanged. Every runaway slave who is caught shall lose one leg or if the owner pardons him shall receive one hundred lashes."

The preacher stopped him. "Then, my Lord, the island of Barbados will be full of the crippled, the dying, and the dead."

Everyone except the planter from Sunbury plantation was satisfied with the new laws.

"They only understand force," Governor said.

"What happens if my slaves are hurt, crippled, or burned so badly, they can't work? I have only twelve slaves. I can't afford to lose any," the planter from Sunbury said.

"Then I will give you a new slave for all your useless slaves," the governor promised. The governor then raised his hand, signaling the end of the discussion.

Mapp was happy with the laws. He hugged the governor as he said, "We have needed these laws for a long time. Our prayers have been answered.

The planter from Saint John who had over a hundred slaves shouted, "Good job, Governor." Another planter expressed worry saying that his plantation had seven slaves and it would be a hardship to lose even one.

The governor also promised him an immediate replacement with a healthy slave for any of his slaves who were no longer of use.

"When will this happen?" the planter asked.

"As soon as the next shipload comes in the governor replied, you can either wait or go on the usual way with slaves disappearing one by one."

Penda, fearing she may be caught eavesdropping, slipped away to Mistress's room. As she walked away, she couldn't stop thinking about the obvious suffering of the slaves on the plantation and it's apparent lack of feeling on Preacher Brown.

Did the words of the Bible, "Let us make man in our image," mean the image that Mapp and the overseer saw? The image of a slave to serve them? And slaves obey your masters, the passage from the Bible preached every Sunday and used as a whip. Was it used to keep us ignorant and saying yes to bad treatment? Where is the passage in the Bible that says love your neighbor as yourself?

Penda couldn't recall having ever heard the words love your neighbor as yourself preached on any Sunday at Coconut Palms. Between the God of Preacher Brown and their main God Dango, she couldn't decide which one of the two was worse than the other.

That night, after they ate, they trudged back to their huts, their spirits downcast. Many of the slaves who had been on the plantation for a long time knew what the governor's visits meant. At the Sunday meetings, they would say that whenever he visited things got worse for them. Penda understood the seriousness of the message, so after the meeting, she walked quickly to her hut, buried her face in her hands, and wept. As she wept, she prayed for strength to last and that she would never lose hope of being free.

As she walked back to her hut that night, she overheard Nehemiah say to Joshua, "She thinks because she in de house, she better than we dat work in de field," and the response of Dorcas was, "We scared of she 'cause she live in de Big House and could carry news of we to mistress." Penda pretended she had not heard them, but their words hurt.

Penda knew that the field slaves fared better than the house slaves because at sundown their work was over for the day. In the big house, the slaves worked under constant observation until no longer needed. The master and mistress made demands on them always. If they failed to be always cheerful or give total service, blows or some other punishment was used. House servants were expected to remain on call even on Sundays for these were precisely the times at which visitors would come to the plantation, and Mistress would have to be served or waited on.

Penda tossed and turned that night until morning. Unable to sleep, she slipped out of the hut for an early morning sea bath. These early morning ventures to the sea had become her one daily pleasure. They gave her a sense of freedom. Each morning, she would leave her hut and walk the quiet dirt road to the sea. At that hour, there would be no one on the path. The sun would be barely visible, giving off a hazy light. Some days she would wade out in the water to her waist height if the tide was receding.

On her way back one morning she met Preacher Brown going to the sea.

"Good morning, Suh" she had been taught to say and had now learned many words from the Bible.

He looked at Penda silently for a moment, then drew out a slow breath. Then he shouted something against the sound of the crashing waves.

Preacher Brown was tall, with brown splotches on his face, almost as if he was turning the color of his name. Their paths came together at the bottom of the trail leading to the sea.

"Last night, Governor read some new laws," he said.

"Yes, suh."

"He means for all the slaves to do as he says, you understand."

"Yes, suh."

"What did the drums say last night?"

"I don't know, suh," she said. Her last response brought no other questions. She was dismissed and she walked off in the direction of the plantation, knowing the drums spoke of a planned revolt.

The governor was cruel, and Preacher Brown knew it. He knew he found reasons to be cruel where there were none. He knew the first laws were cruel even before he added and changed them to be more austere. He knew that laws did not lead to a transformation of a slave's inner sinful state.

Preacher Brown made Penda feel like a human being. The next time they met, she took a risk by saying to him, "Preacher Brown, if you could take my place, would you? Every Sunday, you teach we that God see we as equal."

"Sarah," he said in a tone used with a child, "trust God he has a way of working things out."

She wanted to believe what he was saying, but at that moment, she felt totally empty of trust.

He smiled and took the track on the right. Penda took the track to the left and went back to her duties as Mammy's trainee and Mistress Catherine's personal slave.

Before Mapp's death, Penda had been sent to live with Mammy. She had been on the plantation for three sugarcane harvests placing her age at around seventeen when the decision was made. She was not allowed to return to the big house as Catherine had taken another girl, Martha to be her personal assistant.

"Mammie is becoming old and soon will need attention and the help of someone younger." Mapp stopped her one morning and announced the news to her. The look on his face told her the decision was settled as he turned and walked away.

Penda was to be schooled in the art of delivering and taking care of babies until they were ready for the fields or sold. It was evident that Mammy was aging and soon would not be able to continue as the plantation midwife and nanny.

Penda didn't mind as she thought she would be free from Mapp's midnight visits as he did not frequent Mammy's hut. Penda's possessions consisted of one oversized dress. Mammy had a big book she called a Bible, from which she read morning and evening. Penda hoped she would teach her to read since Odon her friend had been taught by Master.

"One day I will teach you to read as I want you to be able to read to me when my eyes grow dim," Mammy promised her.

So Mammy started that day to teach the girl to read from the Bible. After she mastered the letters, she learned how to put them into words using the Holy Bible. She learned quickly until she was able to do so without assistance, occasionally she worked with Mammy to sound out names that were difficult to pronounce. She was happy when she found her name Sarah, and all the names of the house staff in the Bible.

Mammy got up early before dawn every day. She lit her oil lamp read the Bible, then prayed for all the slaves, the master and mistress, and the overseers. After prayer, Penda was taught how to read. For the first few weeks, Penda disliked the reading sessions. She found the tiny black squiggles and letters strange until, with familiarity and practice under the old woman's tutelage, her stuttering and mumbling became less.

So began a strange new life with an old woman called Mammy. In addition to reading, Penda learned wisdom from her experiences on the plantation and about a new god called Jesus.

"Penda learned from the cook that Mammy used to be important and next in authority to the Mapps. Her main job was to superintend the care of the children in the field, but as she aged, she was removed from fieldwork.

On the first Sunday living with Mammy while the slaves, as was the custom gathered in the common area, Mammy chose to have a talk with Penda. Mammy motioned for the girl to sit down on the tree stump then she served her some food.

"I spend my life on dis plantation, standing indoors and outdoors, in the presence of planters, waiting for dem to decide what they want. Like you, I was at the beck and call of mistress and master, always waiting to fulfill their wishes. I am grateful to master Mapp for sending you here to help me. Master want me to teach you about delivering babies and caring for de children till dey old enough to do fieldwork." Cooking and washing clothes I can still do, don't want no help with them."

"You have children, Mammy?" Penda asked nervously.

"Yes, I had many children for Mapp senior," she answered.

The subject seemed painful for Mammy, so Penda asked for a Bible story.

Bible lessons of Mammy's God who loved the whole world was a concept Penda found hard to believe or accept. Penda found it unprofitable, for with every death of a slave, or a whipping she thought was undeserved, she questioned the love of this God and the sacrifice of His only son Jesus that the old woman spoke about so often. Penda was familiar with the practice of offering sacrifices to her village gods. She questioned if he loved the whole world so much why did he allow them to be brutalized? She began to doubt God's existence along with that of all her gods.

"Every Sunday, we hear the same thing over and over that God is just and fair, and he loves everybody, yet he allows the governor to order indiscriminate, severe beatings because of a rumor. Let us make man in our image. Does this God not care, Mammy?" Penda cried.

"My child, every human being is created in God's image and is different from and above de animals. I believe that as God had plans for Jeremiah while in his mother's womb, he had plans for all of us. Even in this oppressive life, we can make choices. We can choose to hope or give in to despair, to praise instead of grumbling or gossiping, to keep learning and growing, or become dead like de pond with no water. Stop worrying about Master sending you back to the sugarcane fields like dey did with Esther. God has promised to make a way and he will."

Then Mammy prayed and asked God to guide Penda so she would experience freedom one day and have the life he always planned for her.

When Kuba left the morning after the night of their wedding, Penda lay on the mat imagining what it would have been like to get married in the village. Arrangements would have been made long in advance by negotiations between our two families. His family would have paid her family whatever was agreed upon, whether cattle, land, or food. The betrothal could last for months while the girl would have been deliberately fattened up. To be plump was desired. The bride was supposed to be a virgin on her wedding night. Before marriage, their genealogies would be traced by the elders so that a brother and sister would not be given permission to marry. After the wedding, the couple would live in the bride's village.

With a shudder, she turned from contemplating the what-ifs and all possible outcomes. She squeezed her eyes shut and bowed her head admitting to herself that she was sick with fear and apprehension for their future.

Kuba visited many nights after the jumping of the broom, being careful to leave before daylight to avoid being captured. Each time he visited he talked of being free.

"I get to see you once a moon maybe two times, yet when you come, you always talk bout living free."

Kuba pulled her close to him. "I don't want you away from me. Yes, I want to be my own free man. I want to live wid you as my wife like in de village. I know dat you want same ting, Penda?"

"What I want is to forget de life before now and before de ship," she said.

"I will not give up and die, Penda, if we take dis plantation life as everything we giving up. And dis God ting Preacher talk about every Sunday, not true."

"No, Kuba, God of my Bible is real."

He shook his head. "No, Penda, me see it as something to keep de slaves quiet, promising dem land in the sky where no pain. But wat me want is now," Kuba said, becoming visibly angry.

"One day all dis-whippings and dying will end," Penda said as she held on to him begging him to stay even though she knew her request was born of selfishness. She had lost Odon someone dear to her. It didn't matter what Penda said to Kuba that night, he seemed unable to reconcile the childhoods that were destroyed, sold at birth or whatever age the owners decided. He had seen enough in the field, the label 'slave' the children could not have even a stomachache, their focus was not play but learning how to avoid the whip. He knew he wanted freedom.

Desperate to know what Mammy's life was like, Penda summed up the courage to ask her about children the next time they were drying herbs.

Mammy told Penda she had been on the plantation seven sugarcane harvesting seasons when Master Mapp senior forced himself on her. That began his night visits. When she discovered she was pregnant, she was terrified at what could be her fate if Mistress found out. She feared that Mistress would sell her and the child. She would have known the baby was her husband's, so light-skinned in comparison to Mammy's dark skin. Her first child was born in cane cutting season, it was the day that twenty slaves ran away. Mapp ordered the previous Mammy Rose to remove the baby immediately after birth. A boy named Zawadi, which means *gift*. She wanted so desperately to hold him, and breastfeed him, things a mother does to a newborn.

Heartbroken, she was forced to put on a smile like all the other women who had their babies removed and sold to plantations around the island. She had witnessed Dorcas, a washerwoman crying quietly in the field but was forced to put on a smiling face in the presence of the overseer and master. She too experienced the same fears, pain, and anguish of the slave women who had involuntarily said goodbye to their children forever.

After losing her firstborn, she decided not to have anymore. Mammy said to love the baby in the womb and suffer the pain of labor, then have them torn away was unbearable. To prevent another pregnancy, she had been given some herbs from an old slave and these herbs kept her from becoming pregnant for many years. One time, they didn't work, and she had a second baby, a girl she named Aminka, meaning *trustworthy*. This time, Mammy Rose placed the baby on her breast before she cut the cord. The next week, she had the preacher secretly baptize the baby. She was allowed to carry the baby on her back as she worked in the field and in the house.

The lesson for Penda that day was as a slave you learn to live with the uncertainty of being unable to protect your children, unable to keep a promise to be there for them when they need you. The children are lost to their mothers, and so it seems better not to bring them to life. When a slave induces an abortion, what they are doing is trying to save themselves from the torment of losing child after child. Mammy bowed her head, and Penda noticed there were tears flowing from Mammy's eyes.

*****

It was a Monday after one of Penda's reading classes, and the slaves had collected their children, Penda sat down to eat with two of the older slaves Leah and Miriam. After the meal, they all sat at the front of the hut. While the women dozed, Mammy would ask questions of Penda or share her experiences.

"Do you ever think about freedom?" Mammy asked Penda.

Penda shrugged her shoulders not knowing how to answer. She did not know what the word meant, and she did not want to appear stupid. She had heard the word used by the cook, but it sounded like a place. Cook and Matilda often spoke of running away to freedom.

So Penda answered, "Yes, I would like that place where food and huts be better."

"Freedom ain't no plantation, and it sure ain't no place where planter's own," Mammy responded angrily.

"What then is freedom, Mammy?" Penda asked.

"Freedom means not having any white man laying claim to your body, putting you to work in his sugarcane fields, selling your labor and putting the money in his pocket, making you hand your babies over to him at birth, like coconuts in the market or telling you to feel blessed because he feeds you."

"Master never made me work in the fields, and I don't want freedom, me want to go back to the Big House."

Mammy reached out and grabbed her arm in a very tight painful grip, then she raised her hand as if to slap her but halted when Penda screamed out from the pain.

"Freedom means remembering the time when your arm and body did not belong to the Mapp's to punish by whipping, using hot pincers on, or to lay on top of. Freedom is yes and no, two words the master done take away. The only way the master can keep them is to make sure we forget where we come from, the master did not birth us."

The last sentence was said with such force that Penda became visibly afraid. Then in a softer resigned voice, Mammy said. "It means remembering your people back in the village in Africa and where you came from."

"Every slave I see on this plantation looks like someone from my village, they are not, but I know they were created differently by

God. The Bible says in Romans that he has given you and me a skill to do some things better than others, and that tells me that we will never get where we need to go by walking another man's road. That road was cut out for him."

Penda said nothing.

"I have been on this plantation a long time and have seen a lot," Mammy continued. "I have seen people in their first year make every attempt to get back to Africa to warn their people. After that first year, they quickly settle in their minds that there is no going back. Thinking and believing there is no way out of any situation is the way to the grave. Never forget your name and the freedom you had before the white man took you. I learned to read from the master's son, while he was being taught his ABCs, while fanning him in the classroom. Learning to read was perplexing, then one day, it just happened. I never read anything since but the Bible. Mistress knew I was learning to read even though the teacher did not include me in Master Matthew's lessons. It was against the law for a slave child to be taught, but she pretended, and I pretended ignorance.

"The journey from my homeland to this plantation I'm sure was no different to yours. The canoe, the ship, the iron bands around the ankles and necks of the men, the nakedness and humiliation of the slave block, and many women arriving pregnant, and raped by the sailors, things we should try never to forget because to forget is to become careless.

"I was captured at age ten, and you were not yet born when I was taken in the middle of the night. The experience of each slave is the same every time whole villages are captured, the long and dangerous walk to the river, the canoe, and then the months on the big boat at sea, followed by the humiliation and insults of the slave auction. I remember after my capture the villages were set on fire so no one could return, even if some got away. I cannot describe the slaughter of the men who fought with the captors, nor the howling and groaning of the women who watched their husbands killed.

"Absalom was an old slave who became my only friend on the plantation. He would talk to me about his tribe and their superstitions. He also taught me life lessons that I am now passing on to you.

He was one of the wisest men I know on the plantation. He would often tell me that he believed the punishment to slaves for breaking a slave law was aimed at breaking their spirits. We have become full of fear and quick to do anything that we think would bring us deliverance like Kuba, who thinks that stealing guns and gunpowder, even murder would do it. If we refuse to follow God's instructions, we also refuse to receive His promises.

"Absalom looked after me in my early years on the plantation until he couldn't walk anymore. He would talk to me about his village and his dreams of owning land and planting on his return to the Congo if he ever did make it back."

"What happened to him?" Penda asked.

"He is with his ancestors. He died here of old age and never got to return."

That morning, as Penda listened to Mammy, she learned that Mammy's tribal name was Modupe before she was Mammie. When she came to Coconut Palms Plantation, Mistress named her Phoebe. After Mammy learned to read, she discovered her name in the Bible and its meaning—a kind and godly woman.

"Mammy, you ever forget your tribe name or we village, or we ma and ba?" Penda asked, remembering her struggle to remember her plantation name, Sarah.

"Took me a long time to understand that slavery can cause a man or woman to forget who they be. All dem names master give de slaves on dis plantation he take from de Bible."

Penda then shared with Mammy her memory of how she felt on her first day on the plantation when her name was changed to Sarah. She did not like it because she did not get a meaning like she would in Lunda village, but she made herself get used to that name and answer when called by that name."

Mammy said she was never given the chance to keep the children that she had given birth to. When her firstborn was removed at birth, she thought she would die. To date, she did not know where he was or if he was alive, or where her three other children were. Some of her children she said, were sold at four years of age, even though they lived on the plantation until then. What she did to help herself get through the pain, she prepare herself mentally and emotionally for their parting by not getting attached to them. She did not breastfeed them but let another woman feed them.

"The longing to raise my children to kiss and hold them stayed with me day and night. If I had to choose between losing my hands and feet or keeping my children, I would choose to lose my hands and feet over losing them. Here I am now an old woman, and my one and only wish is to see my children and grandchildren before I die. Sadly, it is a wish that will never come true."

"I want you, Penda, to go further than me in learning. No use living in de past. Past done gone, and there be two days. I don't want you to worry 'bout yesterday and tomorrow. Yesterday done gone, and you never can go back to yesterday and change what done already. Nor unsay words you say yesterday. Let we choose to live today."

"But, Mammy, I don't have children, soon me too old to for children," Penda answered.

"Listen to me, Penda, stressing the word listen, to everything there is a season, and a time for every purpose under heaven it says in de book of Proverbs. Don't know what season you be in, but everybody is in their own season. Your time for freedom coming someday. Time not yet ripe, but one day all de slaves be free." Then she prayed asking God to keep bitterness and anger away from the girl and to give Penda the courage and strength to trust him to complete what he started.

After what seemed like another long pause, Mammy continued to speak.

"The wise man or woman is careful with words. Whatever people keep talking about is wat dey have an abundance of. If dey always saying, dey can't then a lot of can't is on dey inside. Your mouth has the power to put you in chains or set you free. Learn to hear, to listen to wat dem saying, but keep your mouth shut. Learn to use your head more than your mouth and you will live."

Mammy looked sad, a look Penda had never seen as she always seemed so joyful. The subject of her lost children had a similar effect on the girl as well. Penda, wanting to cheer her up, thought of changing the subject but now she couldn't think of one. After a while, she talked about missing her mother, eventually ending the conversation with questions about God.

The following Sunday after their talk, Preacher Brown began the meeting with a song, "Abide with me fast fall the evening tide, the darkness deepens Lord with me abide. When other helpers fail and comfort flee, O though who changes not, abide with me."

Oddly, Penda had never heard this song. It talked about the deepening darkness of the failure of people and things to give lasting comfort. It spoke of man's helplessness, of the swiftness of life's little day, the dimming of earth's joys, and the change and decay all around us. She would hear these words in her ear again that night and for many nights as she tried to sleep. Words like, "I need your presence every passing hour, what but your grace can foil the tempters power? Who like thyself my guide and stay can be through cloud and sunshine, Lord abide with me O though who changes not, abide with me—in life, in death, O Lord, abide with me."

What would it be like to have this God always with me everywhere I go on de plantation? A friend who lives with me through storms in the night that make me afraid? In the kitchen, cooking, and when Master in my hut at night? Or when friends like Odon die? Or what would it be like to have a God that I did not have to carry from place to place lasted a long time, who remained the same, was more powerful than all my parents' gods combined and be with me now guiding me through life? Penda mused.

The song brought relief within her though she did not really understand the full meaning of the words. She thought of the words as drops of rain falling on the dry tongue of someone who is thirsty. But something troubled her as she thought of this god. *If I left my gods and followed this Lord that the preacher and Mammy talk about, who would protect me from the anger of the neglected God?* she asked herself, *And where is this God's house? and which God is this? God of the earth or sky?*

Penda became confused as the preacher had just finished speaking of one God, yet he spoke of his son Jesus Christ. He must have a wife then, Penda reasoned within herself, her immature mind greatly puzzled. Preacher Brown continued to speak of someone called Apostle Paul, and how he was bound, jailed, and whipped like them. But no matter how great his suffering, the same Paul wrote that slaves are supposed to do what their masters say. Once Penda learned to read the Bible, she could not understand why slaves depended on Preacher Brown to read. Was it the will of his God that people should own the slaves? if the answer was yes, she reasoned that this new God was not fair.

Some Sundays two of the older women on the plantation would visit Mammy, as her hut was so close to the common area where the services were held. The preaching would be discussed while Penda cooked and served food.

"All he say is bedience, dats all me hear every Sunday, and don't tell lies," Hannah said.

"And don't forget de one 'bout 'you shall know de truth and truth make you free,'" Dorcas added trying to sound like the preacher.

They all laughed.

Mammy in her serious voice said, "Jesus was not speaking of freedom from chains or whips or servants on de plantation, but he was talking of freedom from chains and whips of fear, worry, and anger, tings that keep your mind and feelings tied up."

"Yes, Mammy, me could choose not to worry, but me not free to choose during village raid and capture of me mother and father or how captors treat we on de slave ship. When Master Mapp send me to live wid you or be a maid for Mistress Catherine, me had no choice," Penda responded in a hurt tone.

"I don't think you would know what to choose if Mapp set you free today," a response Mammy meant for Penda.

Silently Penda agreed, admitting to herself that she was unable to form a plan.

The two women then each took turns voicing their fears about how things may change for them as they get older. Then Hannah asked, "Mammy, why you never run away from here?"

"I don't want to be free if we all can't be free," was Mammy's response.

The gray hair pushing out from under Mammy's head wrap and folds of skin hanging from her neck were the only signs that she was aging.

During Penda's second sugarcane harvest, one night after she had settled into a deep sleep, a storm came with strong winds that ripped one of the branches from the roof of her hut. Penda had always been terrified of vicious storms for as far back as she could remember, and to her, they always seemed to come in the night. As she lay awake on her mat, shaking with every peal of thunder and flash of lightning, she wondered how anyone could sleep through it.

At the next sound of thunder, Penda jumped off her mat as the lightning seemed to explode beyond the door of the hut. Everything movable hoes, shovels, and anything that was not tied down seemed to come alive in the wind.

A sudden blast of wind ripped away the burlap curtain that covered the door exposing the interior of the shack to the fierce wind and rain. Unable to ignore the noise, Penda got up and ran using her arms and legs to reach the next hut. The raindrops were hard and painful as they landed on her body. She arrived to find the hut full. Forgetting how afraid she was of the lightning, she ran back out into the night in the direction of Mammy's hut telling herself if unsuccessful, she would try the big house and maybe huddle with the cook and other house staff in the kitchen.

Just as she emerged from the hut, running toward the kitchen, there was a load crash of thunder, then a gigantic bolt of lightning that seemed suspended in the sky for a long time sending what looked like shreds of white light in every direction. Penda screamed and ran back in the direction of her hut, though blinded for a moment by the lightning. Her clothes were soaked, and as the raindrops continued to beat on her face and back, she became confused, unable to remember the way back to her hut. In her partially blinded state, all the huts felt the same as she groped along feeling each hut. The outline of a man's figure appeared out of nowhere. It was Kuba running toward her, he held her till her sobbing stopped, then he guided her to her hut.

"When I see de clouds, I remember how fraid you be of storms and lightning since you a little girl, so me come. But I am fraid de overseer see me, so when rain stop me go." Penda pleaded with him and begged him not to go till morning, but he left after the rain stopped.

Tears flowed down her cheeks as she watched him run away and become enfolded in the darkness. She closed her eyes as memories of the storm on the slave ship returned, the waves crashing against the side of the boat with increasing force, as if a huge fist was pounding angrily against the sides of the boat. She remembered how like tonight she thought death was inevitable.

Mammy talked so lovingly about someone named God, that it made the girl think that since she had left her gods in the village, this God would be a good replacement. The next Sunday after the church meeting while they were sitting outside the hut, she asked Mammy to tell her more about her God and the book she read.

"Where your God live, Mammy? Me want to make one so he protect we in de hut."

"My God is everywhere all time. He in Lunda village now and here on de plantation. His name be Jesus, and you can't make him cause he a spirit."

Unable to say the name, Penda raised an eyebrow and asked again, "What be God name? What be his symbol? What him look like? What kind a wood we make him with?"

"His name is God. He has no symbol, and you can't see him," Mammie responded with a little irritation.

"A God wid no symbol and a God me can't see, but you say him bigger and stronger than moon God or yam God?" the girl asked. Yet as she thought about what was just said, she began to see how their village gods depended on the villagers to move them from one place to another.

Penda was aware that her opinion of her gods had begun to change slowly from the night of the raid when none of them who were thought of and worshipped as being so powerful did anything to free them from capture or defend them on the ship. She had prayed to them and called on them for help until she became weak, they did not intervene on her behalf or stop the hand of the straw-colored men beating, killing, or raping them.

"Penda," Mammy continued, "when I come to this plantation, I used to believe everything you believe about the moon god and yam god, but in this big book, I learn that's not true. There is only one God. I used to believe that once a slave was always a slave, but that's not true either. A long time ago, this book say that God rescued his people from slavery in Egypt, and Jesus died to set us all free from slavery to sin. The yam God and all the other gods never do that. Jesus don't have to be made from wood and be carried from place to place. He be a spirit every place, in Lunda village and here in Barbados at the same time. This God no matter where you are he always there."

As Penda pondered the old woman's words, she thought of her tabletop of gods that her family bowed before every morning. Gods that couldn't make the slightest noise, talk to them, or warn them of the captors who were coming with chains to tie them up and burn their villages; she couldn't remember seeing their eyes opened. Did they know what clothes she was wearing, the age of the people who were worshipping or bowing before them, or the type of offering they brought? She concluded then that her gods were useless since the whole tabletop of them could not protect her family from being captured.

"Think of this, Penda," Mammy said after a long pause," the smallest insect is able to move farther without help than the biggest of your gods."

Mammy couldn't understand how sensible people could talk to a lifeless piece of wood that has hands but can't hold the kola nut you are bringing as an offering to them.

Then Mammy prayed, asking the God who controls the rain that falls and the wind that blows to be a wall of protection around the girl, to enlighten her understanding, that he would cause her to rise above the present circumstances as the eagle does with the storm, and that his hand would shield her from the evil of the plantation.

"The reason I read this book so much is because I'm thankful I learned to read. I know that what is in this book was settled before the world was. God was before my village or yours or even before the world form. These words in this Bible don't change like the clothes we get every year they have never been and never will be. In dis Bible, it says heaven and earth will pass away, but not one word in this book will ever pass away."

"But, Mammy, how your God always watching and let we be whipped till bleeding or let we children go to plantations and we can't find dem or let bad tings be done to we by Master and Mistress?"

Penda was gradually beginning to understand Mammy's God even though she had some difficulty embracing or worshipping a god who watched them whipped, burned, and appeared to her to do nothing about it.

In the summer of Penda's fourth year at Coco Palms, there was an outbreak of dysentery and cholera on the island. Disease spread rapidly in the slave quarters. It was believed that it came from contaminated rainwater in the barrels. Mapp was losing so many slaves that they were being buried two and three to a grave. New cases struck daily as the herbs commonly used had ended. The first man to die was Mosi (Solomon) from Tanzania. He worked in the distillery where they made rum. Men, women, and children were being destroyed by this illness. Fear was visible in the eyes of Master Mapp as the drums continued to announce the coming of more deaths.

A makeshift infirmary was constructed for the sick slaves. When the doctor came his only remedy was severe purging which did nothing but weaken the workers. After one week Gertrude the cook and Abner fell ill so Penda was summoned to help in the infirmary during her afternoons which would normally be spent caring for mistress. She soaked rags in cool water and placed them on the heads of those sick with fever and she spoonfed them tea.

On the following week, Bassa the Overseer was next to fall ill. He was close to death by the time he was brought to the hospital. When his illness was told to house staff, many said they didn't care if he died.

"He pride is wat keep him from going to get help," Dorcas whispered on laundry Monday.

Will the dying never end? What if none of the slaves get better and they all die? she asked herself.

Penda gave Bassa sips of water, not wishing him to die as he had helped to rescue her the last time she tried to run away. At times, he woke up briefly delirious with a fever. At times, he would stare with a facial expression as if viewing a horrible scene, and other times, he would be roasting up with the fever. Then other times, he seemed to be away in another world, staring unfocused out of eyes not seeing her. Sometimes his eyes were pinched shut, his breathing shallow and quiet. Didn't take long before his body began wasting thin.

Bassa's illness made him physically unable to do anything, but it had an unexpected benefit. Because of it, Bassa was rendered weak and ineffective, diminishing his overseer status. He was no longer proud and terrified. A warmth entered their interaction as he began to get better a warmth that previously was unthinkable while he still wielded the whip. From his illness while in a delirious state, she learned his tribal name Mirembe, meaning *one who reigns*. He was from a village in Africa that spoke her language. He was ten when captured, his father died when he was young, and he was raised by his uncle. The story he told as he drifted in and out of consciousness, was like that of any other slave, his capture in the night along with his whole compound, the long walk, and the ship.

Penda was able to piece together a lot of his ramblings like his account of arriving in Barbados feeling overwhelmed by the unknown and the loss of his parents. The hope of escaping was the only thing that kept him alive, so many attempts were made all without success. On his last attempt to escape he hid in the sugarcane all day waiting for the cover of night, but that failed as well when they caught him both of his legs were broken after he was given a severe whipping.

"One word me hear 'sold' me can't bear to hear it. Me have no money, so can't go far, can't runway." Bits of sentences and ramblings continued through the night. He couldn't run away, and he was not strong anymore. His face became hardened, then his body stiffened. He was struggling to speak.

"Me be leader of slave catching, chasing runaways. When me catch dem, me use stretching machine and whip often. Me only think of de masters calling me good overseer. Me kill Odon, de master order it."

"What you say, Bassa? You kill my friend? Why, why? Why?" Penda kept asking but got no verbal response, only Bassa's staring eyes opened in a fixed stare. He seemed totally unaware of her presence.

"Odon ain't do nothing to deserve dat punishment we did to him." He held up his two disfigured hands.

"O God, me hands dey covered in blood!" he screamed.

His screams and Penda's sobbing woke up the infirmary.

"Me wish me could trade places wid Kuba now. When he come to plantation, me treat him bad, so he gets mad and kill me. Me want to see me children. Mapp done sell all dem as soon as dey born. O my sons me want you to live wid me as any father do. It is not as if you dead cause then me take comfort in mourning knowing you back wid we ancestors. De plantation mek it as if you never born.

"On de night Odon dead, me and Master went down de path by the slave quarters. Then me and Master see way off in de distance someone, dragging someting dat look too heavy for dem to carry on de shoulders. As dey come close we see it be Oden dragging what on looking closer be box of gunpowder. Oh God help me, help me he cried. So me send Ezekiel for the pincers wat happen next be fuzzy but after dat Odon lay dead wid blood pouring from he stomach. Me and Zekiel left to dig a grave and planned to bury him as soon as grave finish, but by de time we done digging grave and come for body it gone.

"De days after he dead me feel guilty. Dis secret dat me live wid, mek me alone on de plantation. Me know all slaves hate Bassa. Me liked it at first cause after all me had dem fraid of me. It mek me feel big. Not anymore now me struggle to get tru dis sickness dat bigger dan me."

When Penda came out of the shock, someone was pouring cold water on her face. "Bassa gone to join he ancestors," a woman's voice said. "Death is a door the voice kept repeating, he dead, he free."

Every time Penda thought she was coming to some better understanding of her past, and that she could handle memories from her past, or that the pain of her losses was diminishing to the point where it would no longer intrude on her present, she was forced to conclude that the scars of her past experiences would remain forever, and would be renewed each time she watched a man like Bassa die. Penda wept and ran until she found herself at Mammy's hut. When she stopped weeping, Mammy, in her gentle, voice said, "Penda, you may think that God is silent, absent, or liked de cruel tings Bassa done to we, but no slave master or overseer bigger or stronger than God in dis Bible. He not fraid of any Bassa."

Penda knew that these words were meant to comfort her, but her questions remained. "What God is this that didn't stop her capture? Why did their god Gadon let them be captured and killed without even trying to intervene?"

All the words of comfort that Mammy had spoken to Penda through the years began to bud. Something was convicting her, and everything she had ever believed about her gods started to weaken in the face of the old woman's words. Her beliefs in her gods were not as firm as before.

*****

Several years have passed since Penda was sent to live with the old woman and to be taught everything about delivering babies. Mammy read daily from the Bible stopping occasionally to give her interpretation of certain passages. She continued to teach Penda to read, some days she taught her about herbs and their uses. At the end of Penda's third year, Mammy's health started to decline rapidly. She refused food and spent most of the day sleeping. She no longer attempted to rise at five o'clock in the morning to pray but seemed more withdrawn and into herself.

As she got weaker, Penda noticed that she was not making sense when she spoke. Her thoughts and words became more disconnected when she tried to describe her experiences. Meanwhile, Penda struggled with her own fears of Mammy's death which would leave her isolated on the plantation without her friend Odon or Kuba. The coming Sunday after the gathering, Mammy took to her bed. Penda sensed that Mammy's time to die was drawing near.

The following Monday, a tearful Mammy called Penda to her mat. "I don't want you to cry when I'm gone," she told Penda. "Very soon I will be free from the shackles of this body and will know true freedom. God who led his people out of their bondage will also lead you away from Coconut Palms. When He opens the way run." Sadly, these were her last instructions to the girl.

Mammy's eyelids fluttered, and she opened her mouth as if she had more to say, then she drifted off as her voice faded, and she seemed exhausted with the effort of talking.

She spoke of her husband, Moses, why he had to run away, about her five children with him and four with Mapp, those that survived were sold, how she grieved for them daily, but eventually, "I had to learn to let go of the grief else I would have died." She dozed again, then she woke up with a start. "A man remains the same man before, and after he changes his clothes, so is the Lord who does not change. The plantation will change, but God does not." Penda thought of a hundred things she might have said to her like, "Thank you for all the lessons you taught me. You have been a mother and grandmother instead she said none of these things."

Shortly before darkness came heralding the end of the day, her breathing changed to gasping. Penda's eyes teared up watching Mammy. She wished she could do something, but there was nothing she could do to erase or pause what she saw as her approaching end. Penda sat a little distance away from her as the breathing got louder. She waited for each breath as they grew farther and farther apart.

After a couple of gasps, Mammy stopped breathing, and she heard nothing. Penda ran out the door, intending to get the cook who lived in the next hut, but stopped after two steps, and turned back not wanting her Mammy to be left alone. Penda remained next to her bed, unsure of her next action.

Then Penda spoke to her, "In the silence, I look at you laying on your mat where you seem to be asleep, not moving, quiet, pale. I pray to your God, yet you left me."

She closed Mammy's eyes and mouth as she had seen her do to the dead, and then she covered her body with an old sheet mistress had tossed out. As she covered her, she noticed how tranquil she looked in her final sleep. As the finality settled, her tears flowed for Mammy who she would never see again and for memories of Odon.

Penda stared at Mammy's face for a long time, unable to accept her death as final. While she sat there, she allowed a line of a hymn that she often heard Mammy sing on Sundays and through the week to comfort her. "Change and decay in all around I see, O God, who changes not abide with me."

The news of Mammy's passing was called out to the slaves, and Master Mapp was informed. "We will give her a proper burial," was his response.

Funerals were big occasions on the plantation. Mammy's funeral was held at the graveside. The field and house slaves attended, after which there was food. No one spoke to each other; it was not allowed. On the day of her funeral, Master Mapp led the procession, and all the slaves followed the coffin. Catherine asked to be excused, feigning unbearable grief at her passing, but everyone suspected that she had been drinking. The sermon was delivered by Preacher Brown who praised Mammy for the care she gave the babies and children and for her loyalty to the Mapps senior and junior. She was spoken of on the plantation as a responsible, compassionate Mammy, who could be depended on by her masters and mistresses.

When Mapp spoke, he was unusually lively as he gave some details about Mammy's life. Penda was grateful for this moment of learning about Mammy from one who knew her well. Then closing he said Coconut Palms had met with a great loss in the death of Mammy. "I suppose the plantation will suffer as one like our dear Mammy cannot be replaced. Phoebe was a great woman and will live on in us. She was well-liked by all who knew her. Mammy nursed me as a baby my mother told me and often expressed to me her faith in God. She was aware of her approaching death and conversed freely for an hour before her passing with her young helper. She expressed a hope that she would meet us all in heaven.

After the funeral, Penda remained at the grave site looking at the mound of earth covering Mammy's body, after everyone had left. She looked on the mound of earth as all she had; a reminder that her teacher and model was gone. She stayed behind until it became dark, thinking of their Bible reading times, their many conversations, mainly their last one, and the most painful of Mammy's words, "I'll never see my children or grandchildren," she said, "but tonight I am filled with hope that soon the plantations that take our children will be gone forever, and you, my daughter, will be able to hold and touch your children and grandchildren."

"You going to runaway camp?" Penda asked, not understanding that Mammy was speaking of her death. Mammy did not reply but prayed silently that the girl would be ready for life when the opportunity came.

On the morning of their last Bible reading session, Mammy opened the Bible at Psalm 91. "I want you to read for me." When Penda came to verse 10, Mammy stopped her and repeated the verse, "'There shall no evil befall thee, neither shall any plague come nigh thy dwelling.' I pray that God will guard you even as he guards the birds."

Tears welled up in the girl's eyes as she thought of the word *daughter*. It took her back to the times she had spent with her mother in the field or cooking. A lump rose in her throat as she could not cry anymore, she had run out of tears after three days of crying. Shame filled her, for initially she disliked being forced to live with an old woman. Yet she had received training and discipline from the Bible that at the time, she was unaware would prove indispensable in the coming years.

As she turned to walk back to the empty hut, she looked back at the mound of earth, Mammy's final resting place. Penda had clung to the hope that Mammy would have lived to see her prayers for the girl answered. But now with all her hope gone, she accepted she would never look on Mammy's face again. *How could God love her but let her die?* Penda asked. As Penda turned away, something on the ground caught her eye—a Bible, Master Mapp may have dropped it she thought. She picked it up planning to give it to him at the next Sunday meeting.

Unable to eat the food that was prepared, Penda walked back to Mammy's hut, sat on the mat, leaned forward, propped her elbows on her knees, and stared at the walls. When she could stand it no longer, she pushed herself up and stood looking out the door at the tree stumps where Mammy sat during the Sunday meetings. Then she looked around at Mammy's meager belongings and was overwhelmed by the feelings of emptiness, sadness, and memories while sayings of the old woman flooded her memory. "Don't keep looking back at the past at things that you can't go back and change."

She really missed Mammy, she missed the companionship, and the presence of another person in the hut, someone to come home to at midnight when her duties were done. Now all this was gone. Daytime she thought would be easier as she would have constant distractions at the big house.

CHAPTER 5

After Mammy's death, the house servants gossiped about Catherine's declining mental health. They believed that Catherine Mapp's mental health had started to decline shortly after her arrival in Barbados, and with each miscarriage, it became more apparent. At the sound of the drums, she believed curses were being placed on her.

"It's the drums, the drums are sending curses on me, they are stopping me from having living babies," then she would scream and go into a panic.

Her husband, Master Mapp, had persuaded the Governor to outlaw the drums at Coconut Palms, but the runaways at Bagatelle and the plantations along the coast used them to communicate. The nights were the most terrifying for Mistress, so Penda was moved back to the big house and into her room as a companion.

She wanted to return to England and, in some lucid moments, had asked her husband to do so. Instead, he sent her to the parish of Saint Lucy, to a convent for six months, believing that in an environment of peace and silence, she would make a dramatic recovery, regaining her sanity was short-lived for on her return to the plantation, and she became pregnant and suffered a fourth miscarriage.

"I'm sick," she announced one night, "there are animals in my head, and they run around, but sometimes they sleep. I like it best when they sleep as I get to sleep as well."

During her brief periods of normalcy, she would venture out of her room and have dinner in the dining room with her husband Matthew. Most days, she drifted in and out of lucidity, other times she did not recognize any of the servants including Penda, her personal slave, known as Sarah. Her last pregnancy and loss sent her insane. She could not be reasoned with or calmed. Eventually, Doctor Pemberton the plantation doctor ordered her kept in a state of sedation, saying, "This will pass."

Mistress insanity continued through the planting, seeding, and harvesting of the sugarcane that year. Sometimes missus slept so long that Penda fearing she had died, would stand quietly looking for the rise and fall of her chest. As the illness progressed, she would forget the names of common things like bread, or apples. For weeks missus refused to bathe, despite the heat, her reason, "Water frightens me. What Master called *a passing spell* was wrong; Mistress grew worse.

Three weeks after returning from the convent, Penda and mistress had just finished dinner when the sounds of beating drums were heard.

"What are the drums saying Sarah?" she asked.

"I don't know" Penda lied, knowing they spoke of a planned revolt. Catherine took a quick step forward; suddenly Penda's breath was knocked from her by hard blows to her ribs, head, and face. Staggering backward, gasping, Penda hit the ground, her ears ringing from the blows that came without warning. Penda remained on the ground for a while in immense pain. As she lay there, she heard Catherine calling her name over and over, "Sarah."

Penda kept her eyes closed as Mistress asked her repeatedly, "Why are they laughing at me?"

Penda remained silent.

Penda tried hard to believe that mistress had not meant to strike her. Catherine's hallucinations became more frequent and with them her declining mental health. By the end of that year, Penda had grown accustomed to her mistress illness. Sentences would start and be dropped midsentence or stories told as if her school friends were present in the room. When Penda looked at Catherine, she saw a face different from the face she remembered at the slave auction, or the woman who rescued her from fieldwork after her first week on the plantation. The woman who walked into the kitchen to fetch her then now showed hollow cheeks and sparse hair, an emaciated body, and lifeless eyes.

One year after Mammy's death, Penda was called to attend Governor Goodman's wife in labor. She didn't know if this was his wife's first baby, preparations were made for what could be a long tedious labor. As her steps quickened toward the mansion, though tense, she allowed herself to imagine a healthy baby with a hearty cry and a mother who would be appreciative to the point of appealing to her husband for her freedom.

Preacher Brown had said, "Governor is tyrannical and full of himself." On entering the room, she saw that on a big bed lay a frail woman, not the grand lady of the house she expected.

"We sent for you early," the governor said, "we have heard of your success in the deliveries of babies on the plantation none lost. Also, should we need you in the night, the journey here would not be possible," he added.

Madam was petite; she looked like the baby would not pass through what at first glance seemed to be a narrow pelvis. Madam's face was pale with a tiny nose that seemed out of place. She studied Penda cautiously and her distrust of the girl was obvious. As a matter of fact, she seemed afraid, and her fear and nervousness were palpable. She indicated with one finger that it was her first baby.

Mrs. Goodman was feeling no pain yet, and Penda did not want to spend all day at the governor's residence. She gave no indication that she had the stamina to undergo lengthy labor, but if this was her second or third baby, progress might be more rapid. Penda was shown a place outside the bedroom to sit and wait.

While she waited memories surfaced of women in the village, the stories of their experiences of childbirth. Penda's mother, the village midwife, would say, "It's something you grin and bear until it's over."

A loud moan from Mrs. Goodman halted her walk down memory lane. Penda suggested she walk for a while the same as the village women would until it was time to have their baby.

Mrs. Goodman was getting undressed when Penda noticed she was wearing a large tight band around her waist and stomach. The band had left deep ridges like dents in her abdomen and possible pressure on the baby. She wondered why Mrs. Goodman was wearing something that was most likely very uncomfortable but was afraid to ask a reason as she knew her status did not allow her freedom of such liberties.

Mammy would say, "Dey never accept us as equal."

Madam confided to Penda that this was not the first baby but her third. Her first was a boy who died from a fever, her second was a dwarf born prematurely, she said his eyes were shut tight, and he was tiny with arms like short twigs attached to his shoulders. She said she had heard great things about Mammy but with Mammy gone she had no choice but to have her replacement attend her delivery.

"Have you ever seen that?" she said, referring to the dwarf.

"Yes, madam," she said, holding back the tears remembering some of the disfigurements she had witnessed with Mammy.

Speaking of her abnormal son, she said, "All that day, I held him close to my bosom. The house servants and the doctor thought I had gone insane. I held him until he took his last breath. I couldn't let him die alone."

Two hours later, hearing Madam groaning with each pain, Penda got her back to bed and palpated her belly seeking to locate the head of the baby. Penda's heart quickened; her ears pounded as she was unable to feel anything where the baby's head should have been. She tried feeling again then concluded something was wrong, the baby was lying across.

Beads of sweat rose on Penda's forehead and ran down her body. Her teeth started chattering, and at the same time, urine threatened to flow down her legs. She scolded herself for not examining the madam before instructing her to walk. In doing so, she missed this vital bit of information. She believed this oversight happened as she was overwhelmed with emotion at being asked to attend to the governor's wife. She had assumed that the baby was in the right position with the head coming first. She talked herself into being calm long enough to think of what Mammy would have done then prayed silently asking God to let the baby turn on its own.

"God of Mammy Modupe," she whispered, "I need wisdom now on how to deliver this baby. You know that if anything goes wrong, it is my life that dey take, so help me."

The thought of delivering a baby that was lying crossways terrified her as she did not have to imagine what the consequences could be if anything went wrong. Madame's husband had written the slave laws.

She felt lost at not knowing what to do. Why hadn't the governor used the services of Dr. Pemberton, the white doctor? She knew she had failed by missing the position of the baby. Leaving the room, she called out to one of the older house servants for help.

Between the two of them, they helped Madam get on her hands and knees while Penda rubbed her back. In that position, Penda urged Madam to push down with each pain.

Penda examined Madam again, this time with a plan in mind to turn the baby from inside. On examination, she felt something wet and slippery that throbbed between her fingers. Scared, she let go realizing she was holding the baby's umbilical cord.

I made a mistake in coming, she thought, *but I could not say no to Mapp or the governor.* Then she began to doubt whether this baby would survive or die like the other two.

"You have to use all your strength and push hard!" Penda shouted at her in fear.

Madam tried a couple of weak attempts, and Penda began to fear the worst. After what seemed like hours of Madam bearing down with each pain, she gave one loud scream and delivered a baby boy. Penda's assistant held the baby while the cord was cut.

As the baby reacted to all the new sensations of life on the outside like the bright light of the lamps shining in his eyes and the coolness of the room, Penda completed the cleaning up of Madam.

The baby was cleaned dried and given to the wet nurse for breastfeeding.

When the governor walked in, Penda hardly recognized him because the face she was looking at was younger than the face of the man who had read the slave laws to her on his last visit to Coconut Palms. Everything about him reminded her of a bulldog, the jowls, his furrowed brow, the pale complexion of his balding head the manner of moving, and the growl of his voice.

Today the look of disdain was gone, though unspoken a look of gratefulness was written on his face. She prayed silently that today would stand out in his memory when the time came for her to claim the status of a free woman.

Then she offered thanks to this new God for helping another baby survive the journey called birth.

*****

Today is Penda's last Sunday on the plantation. Fear has gripped her heart about the journey she is about to take. She is to leave on the ship that sails for England tomorrow, Monday. Out of all the house servants, Penda was chosen to accompany Mistress Mapp back to her home in England as her personal maidservant. Some words about God are beginning to make sense, along with a little understanding of his greatness.

As the gathering of Preacher Brown and the slaves sing a mighty fortress is our God a bulwark that never fails, she understands when the last stanza says, "And though this world with devils filled should threaten to undo us we will not fear for God has willed his truth to triumph through us." That day, Penda made a vow to God that she would allow the truths of the Bible to be her compass and guide during this unknown journey and Mammy's God would be hers also. Remembering one of their last talks, "God never tells a lie. There is nothing dat can cause him to change what he say. So know him from de Bible not what preacher Brown say," Mammy counseled.

The young woman quickly packed her things in an old burlap sack she had sewed herself. Looking at her possessions, Mammy's Bible, two of Mistress Catherine's old dresses, one old pair of shoes that were too small, a luxury she never experienced, stockings, petticoats, and an old coat that belonged to Master Mapp. Overhearing Catherine's sister-in-law speak of the weather in England, the cold icy winds and snow, Penda knew she would certainly need something more substantial than the threadbare rags she wore now.

One of the dresses was a dark color with buttons going down the front. The other one was a simple cotton dress. The night before,

Mistress had given Penda permission to visit Mammy's hut as she thought it held sentimental value to Penda and to pack up what was left of Mammy's belongings. But she was to be at the big house to help with any final packing. What Penda did not tell her was that she expected a final visit from her husband Kuba on her last night in Barbados. An extra dose of sleep medicine was given to Mistress. When the girl was sure Mistress was asleep, Penda left for Mammy's hut and her meeting with Kuba. They spent the afternoon in each other's arms as man and wife.

She valued Mammy's Bible more than the clothes she was given for travel, so she decided she would keep it since it belonged to the god that Mammy told her about. Taking her bundle, she walked away from the hut to the big house to await the morning. Unable to sleep from anxiety, fear of the unknown, and thinking of all the what-ifs of the journey, Penda counted every one of the clock chimes that told her the hour.

I will miss that old clock it has become part of my life.

She took a deep breath to steady her nerves and the queasy feeling in her stomach. She had not bled for one moon; this she thought happened because of the preparations for travel and being anxious to leave Barbados for a place called England. The decision for Penda to be the personal companion to Catherine was made by Master Mapp's brother, William, and his wife.

Papers were hurriedly gotten together; the date of travel was set while her heart pounded, and her mind dealt with all the what-ifs of the expected journey." That made her unable to sleep last night.

"This may be too long for you, seeing that Mistress Catherine is taller than you. We get them shortened for you," Eunice said to Penda, speaking of the dresses and petticoats she was given for travel. Then she added, "It's an opportunity Sarah here's a chance to be free if it works out." Penda took the words to mean she had been given an opportunity or chance no one else on the plantation had been given.

Things came to a head one night in July that expedited Catherine's return to England. Just before daybreak, Penda woke up to find Catherine not asleep in her bed. She searched the house and checked the kitchen but did not find her. Then Penda realized she was hearing the crashing sound of the waves, which meant a window or door was open. Penda ran out the backdoor toward the sea just in time to see a head above the water; thankfully, it was low tide. Penda ran into the water, caught Catherine, who was mumbling incoherently, took her back to her room, and got her changed into dry clothes.

The overseer pressed William, her brother-in-law, to have Penda whipped for her carelessness, but the order never came. All he ordered was for the girl to place her sleeping mat on the floor next to Catherine's bed to prevent any further occurrences.

One of the days when Catherine was asleep, Penda was lying on the floor next to the bed staring at the ceiling when her gaze was drawn to a movement on the ceiling. She was watching what turned out to be a lizard hunt.

In Barbados, lizards are small and have brick-colored skin. Graceful and agile, this one scurried effortlessly across the ceiling. It seemed to be moving at a hurried pace. First, it stood motionless as if paralyzed, then suddenly it dashed off as if in a hurry to reach some specific goal it had set for itself. Then it froze abdomen pulsating as if telling the observer that it was exhausted after its last dash, and it was trying to catch its breath and rest before running again.

Usually, evening was the time of day when one would observe the hunt for insects, flies, moths, and mosquitoes. The lizard looked around without moving its head, the eyes appeared to rotate one hundred and eighty degrees. Then spotting a spider, the lizard took off at a rapid speed in its direction.

The spider saw the danger and tried to escape, but instead of running into a nearby crack in the wood, it attached itself to the ceiling with its body hanging down. Helplessly Penda watched the spider get itself into a predicament, trapped. She imagined she saw the spider's eyes darting back and forth, from fear. It was obvious that the spider was coming up short of its goal of freedom. It had exhausted every way possible without success in escaping the lizard. She watched in helpless fear as the spider became a meal for the lizard.

A muscle in Penda's throat tightened, while her heart pounded. Unsure of why a scene of a lizard and spider should terrify her, she tried to figure out the lesson to be learned.

When Kuba visited the night before Penda left for England, he knew that he had taken a huge chance in going to the plantation while the workers were in the field. He hoped no one saw him, and she would be able to get away from work. He told himself he had to see her for the last time. When Penda walked into the hut, she was startled at the sight of his face all bruised with one eye swollen shut.

"What happened?" Penda screamed, forgetting who may be listening and watching.

Speaking rapidly in their tribal dialect, he said, "When I left you, I was unaware of Daniel, the slave catcher, following me." He stopped abruptly.

"You leave me in de morning, Penda," he said, one eye brimming with tears. "I don't want you to go, but I can't do anything. If you stay, you be sold by a new master or bred for more slaves. This way you are safer."

"It's all in God's hands now," Penda whispered.

"Why you talk like this?" he asked.

Angrily, she said, "I want life, freedom, and a chance at least to try." Freedom for Penda at that moment meant being able to sit for a minute, no one claiming her time, thoughts, or the products of her hands, mind, and body.

He could see she was angry, but he kept his voice quiet and appealing when he responded yes.

"Don't you see this as my only way out? Here on dis plantation, I live by Mapp's rules and not my own or the Bible." Her voice broke on this last whispered response.

"You intend to go and leave me?" He sounded like someone who was beaten, tired, and whose mind was too weary to build any response to why she should not leave him. They held each other close, aware of the risks he took each time he came.

"Don't say that, Kuba," she said, reaching out her hand to him.

"I don't even know where you going. You know me must be free to find my way to you."

She thought about his last statement for a while.

Tears flowed from one unbruised eye as he looked at me. He looked like he wanted to protest but knew he had nothing with which to change the outcome.

She took his hand and prayed, "Lord, me 'fraid. Me want to stay with Kuba but you open a way for me. If this be you who make a way, please bring Kuba to England."

"Do you plan to live at de runaway camp all your life?" she asked.

"No, me want be wid you."

At that moment, he reminded her of a trapped bird confined to a cage. He had discovered the camp, but there remained no freedom to be who he would like to be.

"I promise you many things, Penda, but me no have tomorrow all me have is now."

He looked thoughtful, and a long moment passed before he bowed his head. Then he stared out at the cane field directly in front of the hut and mused. *Soon Penda would be on her way to England leaving me behind. No more meeting her after Sunday gatherings. Who will hug her when it storms? When she be afraid. Have I lost her forever? Me can't bear it to see her go.*

Kuba thought of them as children. He would go to her compound with his uncle, the meals she helped cook and serve to them, the games he played with her brother while the men visited. He looked down at his hands, at the weed he had absentmindedly picked on his way to see her. This forced parting agitated him, and he stood abruptly and threw the weed from his hand. He was her husband; he would never give her up. He quietly reviewed the years between being captured, the night of their marriage, and now thinking of her leaving left him feeling tired and fearful. His hands clenched into tight fists. He longed to go with her and protect her. He looked again at the sugarcane fields, and as he looked, 'patience' was the word that rolled over in his mind. He would take lessons of time and patience from the sugarcane seedlings.

In his desperation, he cried, "Earth god, help me find she when time come."

He prayed not as one who believed that any longer but as one longing to be with his wife.

The girl nodded, thinking of the many people who had left the island. "Would I come back?" she asked herself a question she left unanswered. At that moment, I saw exhaustion in him.

Kuba stared at her as she prayed. Then he held her close aware he was on stolen time. They gave themselves to each other that night then he left.

"You asked me what happened after my last visit. The story he related to Penda was that before midnight, she shook him awake telling him to go as she had to return before Mistress wake up."

Unknown to them, the overseer and Daniel watched, but only one of them followed him. The man caught him close to the sea. He felt blows to his head, face, and his ribs. He did not recognize the man in the darkness but remembered hitting the man in the face until he fell over.

Moving cautiously at first a few feet at a time, he moved trying to ease the pain in his ribs. He knew he was injured from the excruciating pain he felt. Walking back to the runaway camp was not only a body challenge but a mental and emotional cleanse as he tried to let go of the anger that burned on his insides toward the plantation and its owners. He tried moving his feet in small steps at a time and resting after each three steps. His breath was coming in gulps, while his fingers were raw and covered with blood. His body ached from the blows he had received.

He decided to travel back to the camp through the cane fields. "Why?" she asked him. The logic behind his decision bordered on the primitive but there was another reason, he wanted to outsmart the slave catcher by going in a direction they would not expect. He remembered that most slaves were caught following the coast. The cane fields offered him the best success. The drums always directed them east, but in his confusion, he couldn't determine which way was east. After going back and forth, he decided to follow his right hand as he had no landmarks.

The cold of the early morning felt as if it was creeping into his near-naked body sending a spasm of shivers through his body.

Each minute, the pain became more intense as he fought to hold on to consciousness. Despite his determination, he began to doubt he would reach the camp before daybreak.

One step in front of the other, his thoughts could not entertain any other activity but reaching the camp. He pictured the slave catchers coming to look for him believing he may have been too injured to get far. He concentrated all his energy on each step.

The ground was rough and uneven, and he soon lost count of the number of times, he stumbled and fell. Each time he got up, he wrapped his arms around his chest to lessen the pain from his ribs. He was blessed in that the darkness started to lighten. He became aware of the blood he was tasting from an open cut on his upper lip, his teeth felt loose, and the pain he was feeling in his loins made it almost impossible to walk without limping. He thought of his wife Penda and forced himself to keep going, barely holding on to consciousness. His right eye was almost closed, his legs cramped from the cold and wet, but he struggled forward urged on by an inner voice that he did not know lived there.

He had lost track of time when his body gave up and turned off his consciousness. He remembered feeling as if numbness was creeping over his body. His courage seemed to have left, and for a moment, he ceased caring. He was ready to join his ancestors.

Just let go, he told himself.

Then two legs were standing in front of him when one minute ago the path was empty. He felt hands rolling him over on his back, then there was a face, gray hair—an old man who resembled his uncle. The man bent over and touched his face.

Kuba made an unsuccessful effort to raise both hands to block what he thought were more blows coming; instead without speaking, but with surprising strength, the man lifted him up and carried him some distance over the hill. Through Kuba's fuzziness of mind, he questioned the coincidence.

Was Penda praying to her god for me? Is my rescue what she would call an answer to prayer or a miracle?

He had fallen within a stone's throw of the small dirt road leading to the runaway cave. The man placed Kuba down after he said something in his dialect. "The knot of death though it be bound with flint can be unraveled by him who knows where the weakest strand lies."

"Wait!" Kuba shouted. "I do not understand!" But the old man kept walking.

That night, dreams of Kuba's first day on the plantation haunted him. In the dreams, he was up before daybreak to the sound of a conch shell and words *get out*. Two overseers who looked like him were using the whip on their bare backs while shouting words he did not understand.

He woke up the next day with a start disoriented in place.

Where am I?

The light was forcing its way through the crack of the hut. Hushed voices were coming from somewhere close.

Oh yes, I'm at the camp.

He tried getting up, but his body ached. After several attempts, he got up, and on blistered feet, he hobbled past the burlap blind and out into the open air.

*****

The carriage lurched as it pulled away from Coconut Palms plantation house. Penda was terrified of something unforeseen that might still happen to prevent their leaving. Soon that fear left, as the plantation gave way to an unfamiliar road. The sun was rising behind the plantation house and a morning mist that covered the yard was now disappearing. Penda kept her eyes open, not wanting to miss anything though the only thing seen was trees, birds, and sugarcane fields that went on for miles. Men, women, and children were already in the fields, their presence sent a shudder and a feeling of sadness for them, knowing they would never leave Coconut Palms plantation of their free will.

The carriage rattled past the Garrison, while Penda tried to file the landmarks in her head, aware she may not see them again. She ached for a last sight of Kuba, unsure of his promise to find her.

Then she prayed, "God, if Kuba not dead, let me see him again, not just for me but for this baby I'm sure I carry."

The buggy passed through a street mistress referred to as Martindales Road, past the governor's house, heading into Bridgetown. Penda could never have imagined she would one day be traveling in the same buggy as her mistress.

As the carriage entered Bridgetown, Penda sat up higher on the bench, having never once visited its streets as that privilege was preserved for select house slaves. The day was different, along the main road there was a lot of activity, women sitting behind small piles of food. Breadfruit and sweet potatoes, she recognized, but not some of the other foods. She stared at the buildings in wonder. Men were walking up and down on what looked like planks of wood carrying packages onto the ship, an activity that reminded her of the way ants carry food to their nests. Somehow it felt strange to her to make this journey, her last through Bridgetown in a buggy, an experience foreign to her life.

She was examined by a doctor, the same one who treated the slaves with severe purging. He listened to her chest, poked, prodded her, and opened her mouth but did not speak during the exam. She felt humiliated as the prodding and poking brought memories and images back of the auction block; women stripped naked and displayed, their mouths dragged open to test the condition of their teeth. The sound of Sarah's slave of Mapp, her plantation name being shouted in the middle of the noise and activity jerked her back to the reality of the moment.

Eventually, permission was given for her to board, and the doctor said, "I have to ensure all servants are healthy to travel on these long journeys."

There was uneasiness as Penda walked up the gangway. Her stomach felt queasy, but this time she ignored it believing the condition came from the black water mixed with the smells native to the wharf. Finally, the gangplank was pulled up, and with it, she felt a wave of apprehension. She consoled herself by saying maybe it represented her last link to the plantation world she had known, which was now being severed. She shuddered at the thought of going to an unknown world but welcomed the thought of freedom and a new life.

It wasn't that easy. She tried pushing the plantation memories and experience away, by reciting words from the Bible, "God had not given me a spirit of fear but a sound mind." That line brought a temporary calm to her spirit, giving some hope again. Having lived through the ordeal of the slave system, she believed that with heroic people like Mammy, she could rise above her temporary status because she had a new God, who she was sure would help her.

The ship sailed on Monday with people who looked as if they were scorched. Penda was leaving behind the hot sun, Odon and Mammy's bodies, the Big House, the old slaves who met with Mammy on Sundays, plantation life, and her beloved Kuba.

As Penda reviewed the events of her last four years, she felt as if a knife was cutting through her soul leaving deep wounds. Images of her father and the men from her village being shackled together brought a hurricane of questions. To quieten her mind, she prayed "Lord, I am yours, and I accept thee as God. I need wisdom to make it through this life. De people that be on Coconut Palms plantation set dem free. Thank You for answering Mammy's prayer for me Amen.

On the ship her sleep was fitful. It took her back to the raid, the slave ship, and the plantation, places she did not want to revisit. It brought sounds of screams, calls for water, words of her captors, and even the sound of the conch shell announcing roll call daily.

The first morning, they awoke to a ringing bell on deck. Penda's duties were outlined to her before leaving the plantation. Helping Mistress with her hygiene and dressing was primary. This morning mistress was calm and agreed to eat in her room. Catherine was asleep one morning of their second week when Penda thought she would use the opportunity to step outside the room for some fresh air. By doing this, she was hoping that the fresh air would ease the queasy feeling in her stomach. Hearing movement in the cabin she went back into the room.

"Where were you?" Catherine snapped. Penda had been gradually weaning her off the sedative that the plantation doctor had prescribed. She was now experiencing longer periods of lucidity, but her periods of anger when they came were very intense.

"You are to stay with me. That is why you are on this ship. Catherine shouted; Penda ignored the statement. The girl on entering the cabin realized the noise she heard from outside was that of her meagre belongings being thrown around the room. As Penda lifted her Bible from the floor, she observed it had fallen open at Psalms 106. Forgetting she was not supposed to be literate the girl began reading aloud, "Remember me, O Lord, with the favor you have toward your people…as a way of calming herself. As she read Catherine's mouth gaped open as if in shock.

"You can read," Catherine repeated over and over. "I didn't know slaves were taught to read," she said, rudely interrupting the girl's reading.

"Slaves be people, Mistress, they be flesh and blood just like you," Penda said, quoting words from the Bible.

Madam became quiet. Penda stopped reading, put the Bible down, and went quickly to her designated space in the corner by the door. After months of these outbursts, she was becoming tired.

After all, she thought, *Now that Kuba is gone…she stopped as the tears coursed down her cheeks.*

A Bible verse she recognized from the Psalms surfaced, "I will instruct you and teach you in the way you should go; I will guide you with my eye." Penda thanked God for his promise of guidance, the sea, its vastness, and the ship moving over it.

Penda remained in the corner away from Mistress until the steward brought her lunch. She was noticeably subdued, and for the first time seemed to be returning to the mistress Penda knew. That evening, instead of the routine screaming, "I'm not hungry," she took the cutlery, held it correctly, and fed herself roast chicken and vegetables.

"Would you like anything else, ma'am?"

"No, thank you, go eat your meal now," she urged.

Servants and personal maids were given cold mashed potato with what looked like ends from plates, a half-eaten lamb chop, or picked over chicken leg.

Catherine's mood remained calm for the first four weeks, but she was prone to bouts of anger. There were no sounds of beating drums on the ship to throw her into an insane crisis. The fourth week at sea the ship met bad weather. Passengers were sick as the ship rocketed violently dislodging mobile objects. By morning, the sea was calm, and Mistress fell into a deep sleep.

"I had the strangest dream Catherine said when she awoke. "I had a baby boy named Nathan. I know he has brothers and sisters on the plantation in Barbados. Do you know them?"

Even if Penda had that information, she wasn't sure if she could trust the new Catherine. She was afraid to share news of her pregnancy with her, fearing Catherine may think that the baby was for her husband who was long dead. Penda was afraid to answer, uncertain of what Mistress reaction may be. Here I am at the start of a new life, yet why be afraid of mistress questions?"

"Ma'am, I do not know of any babies that master is father," Penda answered truthfully.

Mistress looked at her puzzled then continued to stare. It made Penda uneasy, but she remained silent. Mistress finally looked away but did not speak further on the subject.

Penda was left alone with her questions like, *Was this trip a turning point for me? Is this a foretaste of what to expect from Mistress? What's going to happen to me in England? Will I see my husband again?* "O God," she prayed, "help me." Then she silently called out for Kuba. She did not feel that she knew God very well, but she wanted to talk to him the way Mammy did.

In answer to her questions, she told herself, *If I have gained any wisdom from Mammy, it is never live in the future, and don't worry about the past because only God is able to walk back and change the past and only God know me and Kuba future.*

That night for the first time since Mammy's passing, Penda had a dream of her.

Two sugarcane seasons had passed before Kuba got up the courage to run away. He had made many trial runs before that night. He took the time to learn every inch of the plantation. He knew the turns and twists of the stony paths, the fields, and the seasons of the sugarcane. The night, he decided to run, it was very hot and without a breeze. He waited until Bassa had made his last round at near midnight, then he stood at the door and listened to make sure all was quiet. There were no lamps lighted in the huts nor in the big house, so he waited until his eyes grew accustomed to the darkness then he went down the path leading to an alley that ran on the left side of the plantation, a route he had carved out and practiced many times.

After his friend's Odon's death, he was more determined than ever to leave Coconut Palms and never return as a slave or get caught when visiting Penda. He didn't know the circumstances that forced him to return after each practice run, whether he sensed Penda's feelings for him had turned to love or fear. She was not sure if she understood the word as she was only fourteen when she arrived on the plantation. In her immature love for him, she had visualized a different way of life for them, one where they could sit and talk undisturbed. Where the scars of the plantation were forgotten.

Early one morning, a loud shout went up, "Land!" People were rushing on deck to witness. The port at Liverpool England, looked like the wharf in Bridgetown, Barbados to Penda. There was much activity with packages and trunks being unloaded. Small boats were ferrying things and people to shore. A bubble of many words spoken by straw-colored people was in accents that were difficult for Penda to understand. There was a scent on the coats worn by the people that reminded Penda of the small white balls that the mistress kept in her linen drawer. The upper cabins were first off, then the masters, mistresses, and their servants.

William and his wife, Catherine and Penda stepped off the gangway into dim sunlight. There was a cold wind that seemed to cut through the fabric of her clothes causing numbness in the part of her body where it touched. The trees had no leaves, just bare branches with a few birds sitting. She had never experienced this type of cold that made your bones, ears, and hands hurt until all feeling was gone. To Penda, it was a strange world.

Catherine was very quiet in the hustle and bustle. William arranged transport; an open cart pulled by two horses. The rattling of the cart and the clip-clop of the horses seemed to lull the four of them into a kind of sleep.

If only I could write Penda thought, there's so much I would share with Kuba, but she was thankful to Mammy for teaching her to read. In encouraging Penda to read, Mammy would often say if you can read no one can have you carry your death sentence like Uriah, Bathsheba's first husband in the Bible.

A man brought the valises and trunks to the door of an inn William had secured for them. At the inn, the four of them were met by a plump older woman.

"Are you looking for rooms?" she asked with an accent Penda struggled to understand.

"Yes please—one double and one single" William answered.

"For how long?" asked the man.

"One night," said William.

That settled, the luggage was taken up the stairs by a young man who seemed to appear out of nowhere. Soon they were drinking cups of hot tea that had been offered. Sugar was added and something called milk that gave the tea a spice color and a chunk of bread covered with a sticky orange substance.

"Thank you," William said, adding, "my sister tires easily, she has not been well and would like to lie down."

"Sure" the woman replied. Upstairs Penda helped Catherine undress for bed. Laying on the cold floor next to mistress bed, Penda waited for her to fall asleep. She had difficulty finding a comfortable position to sleep. She decided to use the time to reflect on the past two stages of her life, reaching a conclusion that the new God she had encountered made it happen.

She continued to be amazed by the drastic change in Catherine, who was very quiet, her face relaxed. She wanted to believe that the prayers offered up to God had been answered and yet she struggled at times with the thought of totally abandoning her gods. Penda was still reluctant to part with the sacred tribal taboos she had been taught, as Preacher Brown's god always seemed silent. She believed he looked away when the slaves were being whipped, killed, or forced to lie with them as a wife should. He looked away when the babies born of those unions were sold for money to plantations far away from their mothers. His ears seemed shut to the suffering of the mothers and children as they were wrenched apart, their cries for mercy ignored. The girl's internal debate continued long into the night after Mistress fell asleep.

She gave thanks to the Lord for keeping them safe on the ship. Then she thought about the words of the song, "A mighty fortress is our God," she heard it sung at the last Sunday meeting on the plantation.

> A bulwark never failing, our Helper he amid the flood.
> Of mortal ills prevailing.
> For still our ancient foe, doth seek to work us woe.
> His craft and power are great and armed with cruel hate.
> Did we in our own strength confide our striving would be losing.
> Were not the right man on our side, the man of God's own choosing.
> Don't ask who that may be, Christ Jesus it is he.
> Lord Sabaoth is his name, from age to age the same.
> And he must win the battle.

Penda began to understand what a fortress meant—a place that is impossible to penetrate or enter. If God promised to be that to her, she would trust Him. She thanked him for keeping her safe from the mystery sickness and fevers that took the lives of many on the slave ship, for keeping them alive who made it to Barbados, and for protecting her from being raped as she witnessed on the boat from Africa. Next, she thanked him for his Word that assured her his promises are not seasonal like the sugarcane harvests and hurricane times once a year, neither do they rise and set like the sun and moon. The wealth of planters does not influence its power. She thanked Him for his Word that is without bounds, for its omnipresence whether awake or asleep, on the plantation, boat, or in England.

"How precious are your thoughts unto me O God, how great is the sum of them.

In the book of Kings in the Bible, it says, "Blessed be the Lord that hath given rest unto his people, according to all he promised; there hath not failed one word of all his good promise…

"Mapp promised me freedom but drew the line somewhere, but you God promised your son and you did it. I don't know what it is like to give up a child as I don't have children yet, but you gave your only son; that is beyond my understanding.

"Mammy was proof of god's unchanging faithfulness. One of her last words to Penda was, 'God never stoops to a lie.' There is nothing that could cause him to go back or change what he said as that is not his nature. Furthermore, the All-Powerful God can do all he promises. We sometimes promise to do something but find we can't do it 'cause we be human, and can't see the future and fence that lie ahead. So the promise fails because we be human."

Finally, Penda prayed that the unmistakable friendship and confidence Mammy had with God she would experience in England.

As she fell asleep that night long after Catherine, she thanked God for blankets, for a room with walls not made of mud, for cups and a bowl not made from a calabash gourd.

Lastly, she thanked him for sugarcane and sugar. She saw God's plan now for without the sugarcane and its demands for labor she would not have experienced Mammy or be brought into a knowledge of her God.

The last two lines of the hymn were all Penda remembered before she finally fell asleep.

"And though this world with devils filled, should threaten to undo us.

We will not fear, for God hath willed his.

Part 2

UK

God's plan of blessing for everyone is different.
His designs are never hurried.

—Author

CHAPTER 1

The girl was thrown out of number 25 Greystone Manor into the night—a cold windy and rainy spring night. The wind was blowing so hard that it blew her coat open, allowing the rain to soak the front of her dress. The wind tugged at her head tie, threatening to blow it off. She struggled to carry her few belongings and keep her coat and head tie on all at the same time. Penda could not believe that Catherine Mapp had thrown her out at a moment's notice, believing that she was pregnant by her dead husband, Matthew. He had been dead for four years.

That Mistress Mapp could do this with no reason. Her heart was hard for the girl to comprehend. There she stood in the doorway of the house, trying to come up with a plan. She thought of going back to the house and pleading with Mistress in the hopes that she would repent throwing her out in such inclement weather and that she might allow her to stay in the cellar overnight. But the house remained dark. She didn't know where to go to the village as she had only been in the village for six months. Where could she ask for accommodation?

"It would arouse too much curiosity, too many questions if she told them where she lived," she self-reasoned.

She imagined people asking, "Why do you need a room?" With Catherine Mapp living in a big empty house alone?

After what seemed like a long time of answering and discarding each thought, she decided to go to Southampton as she had learned from the weekly newspaper that there were pockets of black servants there. She decided she would become a nurse maid, but she wanted her baby when born to be with her. She knew there was a railway station but was unable to estimate its distance or to ascertain if trains ran at that night hour. She could not think of what she could offer for a room at the railway hotel since she had no money. Therefore, the idea of a room at the railway hotel was discarded.

The thought of walking a mile of twisting dark lanes on a rainy night daunted her, but even that was preferable to possibly being sold again. She pulled her coat tightly around her tummy, which was beginning to rise, and set off in the direction of where she thought she would find the railway station.

She left Pleasanton village, following a footpath that was dotted with light from occasional bursts of lightning. She had gone about one-quarter of the journey when she felt fear rising. She began to chide herself for embarking on so dangerous a journey, not to mention impulsive. The rain fell more heavily, and the wind played havoc with her clothes. She couldn't see where she was going, and more than once, she stumbled into mud at the side of the path.

It became a question to herself, "Should I turn back?" Yet she kept going until, with each stumble, she reached a place in her mind of no return.

"Why should I go back?"—and to that question, she felt a rush of obstinance. "I will never go back," she told herself. "I will never go back to 25 Greystone Manor, never."

Common sense told her that Catherine was not who she was in Barbados. She had returned to England and, on regaining her mental faculties and orientation, discovered that all the money Matthew gained from slavery had been squandered or gambled away. She would keep Penda on as her personal servant for free labor. When the girl's pregnancy was confirmed, Catherine took it as an opportunity to get her out of the house.

As Penda walked and conversed with herself, the journey became less frightening. Sometimes she prayed.

"I expected Mistress to be more understanding. Did she forget the care I gave her or the years I waited on her in Barbados? Was I really her property?"

Before a month had passed of living with Mistress Catherine in England, her title had moved from slave to servant as a pretense to hide the scorn of slavery. Her duties were not modified from those of the plantation.

She got up with the dawn on those mornings that always seemed like night. She was ordered to scrub the floors as many times as Catherine wished. The most difficult thing initially was getting used to English time. However, her life was now lived in an orderly monotonous way until the night without warning she was told to get out.

Despite Penda's resentment over the situation, she could understand Mistress Catherine's attitude. She had been widowed, childless, and was faced every day with a pregnant servant who she was sure was carrying her husband's mulatto baby.

It took Penda a long time to decide she was having a baby. Mammy had tried one day to teach her about this matter, yet she remained ignorant. Mammy had tried to enlighten her about sex, but Penda was shy, and the subject was dropped.

This was not something mothers discussed with children back in the village. Penda had never been able to depend on the regularity of her cycle since it started at thirteen—the year before she was captured. Any kind of upset like a cold could throw her cycle off. But even though she knew her fate—morning after morning on the ship, waking up to the same awful feeling of nausea—she was glad that Catherine slept her drug-induced sleep until afternoon.

Penda had been married two years, and it seemed had not become pregnant in that time probably because of the infrequent night visits of Kuba, her husband. Before leaving for England, his visits had become more regular almost nightly.

Penda lifted her face to the rain and began to pray, "Lord of Mammy's Bible, hear me. I belong to you. I see where you didst not let de children of Israel be alone. You say thou art with me all de time. I want to trust you now when it looks hopeless. Mammy's God, why bring me here to England to be without a place to live? I don't know what a broken heart feels like, but David, in the Bible, write about it. Right now, my heart feel as if it will break.

Losing Mammy, Odon [my mother], and Kuba [my husband] is enough to do that. Lord, I don't know why I am here in this country, but I want to believe thou art working something out. Thou promise never to leave me. Please send help 'cause I scared. On the other hand, Lord, I fraid of freedom. I have no experience of it as Mammy told me. I'm wet and I'm cold. Please send me some help. Amen."

She struggled to remember the ways God had rescued her from being molested on the boat or from Mapp during night visits and from the torture that she could have suffered at the hands of Bassa the Overseer after she ran away.

She told herself that memory is a horrible thing to lose, especially if the memory is of God's goodness, grace provision, and protection. Tears were raining down her face as her prayer trailed away, and slowly, she turned her head to listen. Yes, she heard a faint sound of clip-clop. It was a distinctive sound she had heard on her first trip to the parade, and she knew it was made by horses' hooves.

As she walked, strong winds whistled and howled while the boughs of the trees creaked and groaned like a human in pain. She became more afraid of the strange noises filling the air than the driving wind blowing into her face, slowing her footsteps. Her feet felt like lead had been built into them. She tried not to think or remember. "Just put one foot in front of the other just keep moving," she coaxed herself. With each step, she wept.

At regular intervals, she imagined she heard footsteps; and on each occasion, she was mistaken. There was no one on the track with her. She was not sure how far she had gone when she was sure she heard the clip-clop of horse's hooves—a sound that became clearer and louder until in a frightened panic, believing something bad was about to befall her, she stepped off the track into the wet mud to hide behind a bush. Clip-clop went the horse's hooves, clip-clop past her. The rider of the horse was a man she did not recognize in the dark. A few clips further, the horse and rider turned around and came back slowly as if checking something out.

Robert Parker from Downham Manor said goodnight to his friend at the pub. They played Game of the Goose all evening. Robert had spent this occasional evening playing with his friend Spencer and decided to leave after a long session and a bottle of whisky between them. He was feeling warm from the whisky and the coal fire he had sat next to. He did not feel the hard rain, so he moved Belle, his horse, along the path at a slow pace. The wind kept blowing the lantern hanging on the buggy side to side. He must have been lulled into a sleepy state when suddenly he thought he saw what looked like a human face. Initially, he thought it may have been an illusion caused by the overconsumption of whisky, and so he kept on.

He had gone a few more paces when he thought to himself, *Was that a human face I just passed?* He turned Belle around reluctantly, and with difficulty, the track was narrow for the wheels of the buggy.

Penda gave a sigh of relief as the horse passed her. However, she saw it turn around and head back in her direction. Trembling in fear, she tried to fully conceal herself behind the bush.

"What are you doing?" asked a man's voice. "Are you in trouble?"

"No…no," the girl stammered with fright, hoping the man would go on.

"Well, this is no place to shelter," he said sternly.

That was true because the bush did not provide adequate cover. She was thoroughly soaked.

"Where are you going?"

"De railway station," she said.

He got down from the buggy while Penda waited, terror-stricken. He lifted his lantern to her face, wondering why she should be out on such a wild stormy night. Whatever her story, he would get to it later.

"You better get out of the mud," he said as he extended his hand. "Give me the bag."

Trembling, she handed him her tied-up bundle and allowed him to help her up in the buggy.

"Are you meeting someone?" he asked again.

"No, suh, me alone," she said.

"Then you should have waited until morning," Robert said. The girl remained quiet.

"I can't leave you here," the man said, "nor can you stand here all night getting soaked."

"I alright," she said hastily. "I can get to station."

It didn't take her long to give in and accept the ride he was offering. Penda was still afraid because she had already experienced one potentially destructive shock earlier in the night. She had learned how to keep her ears and eyes open on the plantation and knew the danger of speaking to an unknown white man—most dangerous to go anywhere with them and worst at night. Her greatest fear now was being sold again. Penda sat next to the man on his buggy. With every step the horse made, she became more nervous. She had heard of women being raped, and she feared this might happen to her too. They made their way down a deserted road that wound through trees. Then the road turned, and she could make out some small buildings. Abruptly, it stopped at a house.

What seemed like an eternity of cold and wet came to a sudden halt when the horse stopped. She looked up and around, seeing nothing but darkness.

"Is this be the station?"

"No," said the man. "My house."

"But I want to go the station," the girl said, all panicked.

Lancashire, he recalled, had started having an increasing number of negroes as servants and stable boys.

He tied up Belle and took the Bible and the bundle she held.

He would inquire later about her literacy status but not now. He unlocked the door and went inside, lit an oil lamp on a table, called her in, and announced he was going to put Belle in the stable. He left, closing the door behind him.

The room got warm while Penda was left shivering in wet clothes, worrying about what the man intended to do with her. She felt defenseless, out of place, and frightened by the emptiness. As she sat there waiting for him to return, a discomfort indefinable crept over her, and at the same time, she shivered from a sensation of cold from the wet clothes. Penda shifted uneasily on the chair; the discomfort mounted in her until it ceased to be discomfort replaced by fear.

"Why am I afraid?" she asked herself. She looked about her. There was nothing to be afraid of, but she clasped and unclasped her hands as she struggled with an urge to run.

Robert knew from looking at her that she was a servant. Watching this young girl, the memories of his years as a slave owner came rushing back. She was gaunt but walked upright. He noticed that her eyes were dark when he forced her to raise her head and look him in the eye. It was too late to erase the slave trading days, but he could accept that regardless of skin tone. All men were made in God's image.

What troubled him was why she was without her mistress. He did not show haughtiness but talked to her in a natural tone.

While he was gone, Penda relived the Monday morning when she was summoned by her mistress to the library and given a list of groceries to bring from the village shops. When she closed the gate that first morning, she felt strange in a sea of white faces.

"Am I being stared at? Do they know that I am a slave?" she asked herself. When she reached the corner of the road, she had a desire to run back and bang on the gates. She felt fear and loneliness, having never been by herself, not even the weeks spent on the ship.

She was surprised at the insight she had gained into human nature just by observing the lives of the slaves on the plantation and the way her years of confinement plantation tutored her mind a little to a certain stage of reasoning. This change had happened so discreetly and unnoticeably that, while it was happening, she was unaware. She knew she thought differently to others, yet she admitted to herself that she was afraid now of the unknown.

This fear was nothing compared to the fear she felt facing a table full of laughing faces and questioning eyes at the slave auction. She was given the directions in writing for which she thanked God for being taught to read and prayed that she would find her way there and back. She studied the names of the streets as she walked, committing them to memory for her walk back to the manor.

She turned right, then left, then left again, and there it was a row of shops. She passed a great fruit shop, where a waft of air brought a scent of ripe bananas, oranges, and lemons. She was so lost in her reverie that she did not hear Robert return or know how long he had stood there. He was studying the girl in front of him with interest, noting something about her despite the ill-fitting, shabby brown coat. He felt disposed to help her by giving her shelter.

Penda looked down at her shabby clothes—half in shame and half in surprise that the man had not let it hinder him from treating her as a human neither had he taken advantage of her. Mr. Parker, in his apparent acceptance and care of her, nourished a part of her that corresponded with the words of her Bible: "Love your neighbor as you love yourself." The thought of being tossed out did not seem so bad after all, and hope was being birthed in her heart that, somehow, she would find a way out of her predicament. As she closed her eyes to sleep, somehow Robert's kind eyes mingled with her sleep and seemed to promise her relief from her present anxieties.

"Tea?" he asked.

"Thank you, suh," Penda said.

He glanced at her in surprise as she spoke well for a slave and her manner was not that of a servant. Most of them he had encountered were illiterate.

Penda got up, removed the wet coat, and offered to help the man.

"No, just warm yourself," he said firmly.

Young, Robert thought. *Twenty-one maybe. She doesn't look like one of the servants he had seen out with their mistresses.*

Penda stole a few shy glances at him as he busied himself with the tea. He was a big man and tall like Master Mapp, she thought, with a brown face like the plantation owners she remembered from Barbados.

He brought her a cup of tea and inquired if she was hungry. She was hungry but did not want to say so. Such care was very foreign to the girl who only knew orders and leftover food from the table. Penda's mouth drooped a little as she remembered. Then a glint of tears gathered in her eyes before she held her head down as per plantation protocol. She kept her eyes on the floor.

Why be thrown out this time of night in this weather? he asked himself. He wondered and guessed what may have gone wrong. He was familiar with the plantation system as he was a planter in Jamaica and had done things that he was now ashamed of, like having babies with slave girls and selling them off at birth while witnessing the mothers struggle not to show sadness. He was now a changed man, following his life-changing experience of becoming a Quaker and an abolitionist.

His thoughts and questions continued. *What had she been up to? Had she been a maidservant?* Initially, he thought the man of the house had been responsible for her condition as was common.

She kept her head down and nodded in answer to all his questions.

"And you have nowhere to go?" he asked.

Penda shook her head from side to side, determined to keep back the tears that were fighting to come out.

She accepted the pastry and tea he offered.

"Where were you going by train? I thought you said London. Who do you know there?"

"I met two women on the ship who told me the place they were going to in London. They could not write, but I memorized it."

"Go to them in the middle of the night? What a foolish idea, not to mention your ignorance of London. The best thing is to sleep and set out tomorrow morning," he added as an afterthought. Robert could see the fear in the girl's eyes, and to allay her fears, he assured her he had no wife and he would not trouble her. These words had the opposite effect, because instead of calming her, she became visibly afraid now, knowing she was alone in the house with him.

"Why you bring me to your house?" Penda asked, shaking.

"I have seen slaves before. You had nowhere to go."

"What you plan to do wid me?

Parker's brow wrinkled as if reading her thoughts, and he said, "I am not going to harm you. I don't consider myself your owner. You are free, but it all depends on who you are running away from."

Penda remained quiet for a while. "So can I go in the morning?" she asked.

"I won't stop you from going again, but I might try to convince you to pick a better place than London."

He was right about that; she had no idea where she would go in London.

He showed her to a room, then brought her some clothes that belonged to his mother, a hot water bottle and sheets for the bed, and instructed her to lock her door.

"Have no fear. You are safe." He thanked God that she was fortunate to have been found by him as he considered the many cruel things that may have befallen her.

"Good night. What is your name?" he shouted as he turned back.

"Sarah, slave of Mistress Catherine Mapp," Penda responded.

"No," he said firmly. "What is your name? Can you remember your name?"

"Yes, suh, my name be Penda."

"Mine is Mr. Robert Parker. Good night, Penda." He went out, closing the door behind him. Robert and Penda knew this was a social breach that would never have been admitted as acceptable.

Penda waited until his footsteps got less and less as he descended the stairs, then she began to make up the bed by the light of two candles—a practice like that of Mistress. Interestingly, she thought, *I didn't have a room in that big house but a cot placed outside her room where I could be roused at any moment.* Something about this house—an atmosphere maybe—aided in reducing the girl's feelings of uncertainty and despair.

She got changed into the nightdress, put her damp clothes over the back of a chair, checked the door, reassured herself it was locked, and got into bed. She was tired and very frightened. As tired as she was, she couldn't fall asleep immediately. She kept thinking of her past hours, her mistress's reaction to her swelling belly. As she stared at the shadows created by the candles, the events of the night at Chigwell Manor rolled over repeatedly into her mind. She was wearied by the problem that had been pressing on her brain, yet she felt hope growing on the inside that something good would come out of her experience. She offered thanks to God for answering her prayer and sending Mr. Parker to rescue her and give her shelter. Then she reviewed all the promises of the Bible she could recall and drifted off to restless sleep, filled with bits and pieces of the evening—Kuba holding her and Robert bringing her to his house.

Penda struggled to forgive Mistress Catherine for throwing her out. She thought it a cruel act, considering she had accompanied her across the sea and knew no one in England. She tried to forget the words used to describe her and the unborn baby, mistaking it for that of her husband who had been dead for two years. She let some memorized Bible verses be the last thing to occupy her mind before blowing out the candle.

Penda awoke to tapping on her door. She could not remember where she was until Robert's voice reoriented her memory to her whereabouts.

"I'm off to the farm and be back later. You can cook yourself some breakfast."

She heard him go downstairs, and she listened for a door closing that would tell her he was out of the house. She went to the window to watch him leave but saw nothing, realizing her room was at the backside of the house. She turned back again and listened carefully as her suspicion heightened that it may be a trap. She heard no sound. She decided to work on a plan of escape, but instead, she got her Bible out, and it fell open at John 14. Her eyes caught verse 18: "I will not leave you comfortless; I will come to you." She continued reading until verse 27. "Peace I leave with you, my peace I give to you not as the world giveth, give I unto you. Let not your heart be troubled, neither let it be afraid."

She closed the Bible, and upon opening it again, she realized she was in Deuteronomy 31:6. "Be strong and of good courage, fear not, nor be afraid of them, for the Lord thy God, he it is that doth go with thee, he will not fail thee, nor forsake thee."

Encouraged by the thought that, no matter how terrifying her circumstances or how powerful her mistress appeared, she would not be frightened but would trust God's word. Then she prayed, asking the Lord to keep her from giving in to bitterness or wanting to pay her back for what she did. She wanted to be obedient to the Bible that instructed her to love her neighbor as herself and, in all things, to give thanks—words she heard repeated every Sunday on the plantation. So in obedience, she thanked him that she was thrown out for the baby in her womb. She thanked him again for Mr. Parker and looked forward to the end of this situation as he must have a reason for her trial. As she closed her eyes to sleep, somehow Robert's pleasant voice and kind eyes mingled with her sleep seemed to promise her relief from her present anxieties.

The following morning, after Penda washed and dressed, she went downstairs to prepare breakfast for Mr. Parker, trying to remember her cooking from the village. She had helped the housekeeper at Catherine's on many occasions prepare meals. She hoped Robert would not think her a *slut* as Mistress Mapp called her the previous night, adding, "Go and birth Matthew's bastard somewhere, not in this house." As she rehearsed these words over and over, her heart beat painfully like the throbbing she once experienced from a boil. She didn't know what the word meant, but the tone of voice and facial expression used as she spoke convinced the girl it was something bad.

At the foot of the stairs, Penda caught sight of herself in the mirror and stopped for a minute. She looked at her eyes, which were dry and dark like an old woman's, and her face that looked so much older than her years. When she looked at her face, she thought of words in her dialect that would accurately describe what she saw but was unable to do so.

Robert Parker couldn't sleep that night because he was thinking of the girl he had taken in. Early the next morning, he went into his library and sat at the desk, intending to review the list of names of slaves arriving the coming Friday. He sat still for what seemed a long time, looking out the window at the daffodils but not seeing them. His thoughts turned to the girl. His thoughts were interrupted by the sound of sobbing.

Mr. Parker had left on the table eggs, bacon, bread, butter, tea, and preserves. When Robert got ready to leave the house for the farm, he stood in the kitchen for several minutes, looking at the chair where the girl had sat the previous night. There was something in the face of the girl that left an impression of character and a struggle with forces of which he, in his sheltered life, had only a vague conception. It left him with the feeling that she was, in some ways, stronger in character than she appeared. She had a bit of time before his return, she thought, so she began to look around the house, being careful not to touch anything. Her treasured discovery was a room with many books and a large Bible sitting on the table.

Robert returned to the smell of bacon, toast tea, and just the eggs to be cooked.

"Give me two eggs," he ordered.

As he washed his hands, he studied her covertly. When he sat down to eat, he invited Penda to sit. Then she enquired if everything was to his satisfaction. Despite the invitation to sit at the table, she made no movement to obey him as an action as that would cause her to violate a protocol that was on a level with looking a white person directly in the face. In the daylight, while Mr. Parker gazed out the window, he looked bigger than he appeared that first night. "Maybe it was his coat," she concluded.

"It's good. Where's yours?" he asked.

"Here, sir," Penda said, showing him one egg on the plate.

"That's not enough for a bird, and you are with child," he answered, offering her another egg.

"About this being thrown out of Greystone Manor, who tossed you out?" he inquired.

Penda was silent for a moment, afraid of where his questioning could lead, then remembering how glad she was at his treatment of her last night. She answered, "My mistress Mapp."

"Why?"

"She believes I am pregnant for her husband who died on a plantation in Barbados two years ago."

At that, he laughed. It was a phenomenon that piqued his interest yet obviously embarrassed the girl. He looked away as he drank his tea, giving her time to recover. He studied her for a while, then asked, "Well, what brought you to Lancashire? And what happened at Mrs. Catherine's?" He pressed her until, with downcast eyes and in stops and starts, she rehearsed her life at Coconut Palms plantation in St. Phillip, Barbados, her marriage, and how she became Mistress Mapp's nursemaid. Robert processed all that she said. He believed her.

"Now listen up, it is obvious you are expecting a baby. So tell me what really happened last night." The question was raised again.

His manner gave her reassurance and comfort, so she told him the whole story of the previous evening, faltering and hesitating occasionally. After giving her account, they both became quiet, and each seemed engrossed in their own thoughts.

"Do you still want to go to London?" was his final question to her.

"Not really, I'm frightened but don't have another idea." She thought of asking if he would help her find another position like nursemaid or personal servant.

"Stay here and think it over," he counseled, hoping he could keep her as another help to his housekeeper who was visibly aging. The farm was getting busier, he thought, and every extra help would be welcome.

"My housekeeper is away for the week, so you can stay and cook the meals."

"Thank you, sir."

When he came home for lunch, he spoke little while he ate. Afterward, he inquired what she had decided to do.

"Sir, I need a place to stay, so when I have the baby, I can take care of her."

"You said 'her.' How do you know that?"

"I am hoping for a girl."

"Where do you intend to leave the baby? I take it you will accept the job of housekeeper if, after I speak to your mistress, we can come to an agreement. I will go see her tomorrow."

With that settled, he reached for his pipe and began to fill it. Penda felt dismissed by this action, got up, and began washing dishes. The topic of her pregnancy or how she would manage never came up again. He determined that he would do for her what he was too much of a coward to do for the number of his children gotten from the slaves. After all, it was his seed he disposed of by sale.

Robert continued to observe Penda. For all her shyness, he saw someone who—though it appeared much of her humanness had been stolen from her, unlike many of his slaves in Jamaica—displayed a sharp mind of her own. He was surprised at her level of maturity though her naivete in other things amused him. It would be interesting, he thought, to mold and teach this immature mind. There were some things he decided she needed like some new clothes; to be taught to speak English, not that of the bible; and the correct way to use knives and forks. She also needed to be taught table manners. English customs he thought she would learn easily. Shrugging, he thought, *People mature quickly in such surroundings as a plantation. In fact, they must if they are to survive.*

She was a reasonably good cook, not great—that was to be expected since her experience was as a nursemaid, a servant. He liked the way she expressed herself using words from the Bible. He had given himself time to think over the situation. He would go to see Catherine and maybe try to buy from her the girl's freedom. That night, he prayed, asking God for the wisdom to speak to Catherine in such a way that she would be willing to release Penda to him.

Penda went to bed that night in a confused state of thankfulness to God for his provision, protection, and for the man who rescued her even if things didn't work out. She threw herself on the bed and indulged in bitter tears that were not quenched by the realization that she looked forward to this journey. She couldn't help reviewing the evening while trying to make sense of her eviction. A series of questions were thrown out and answered by Penda in a long conversation. *To be put out on the street in a strange country*—a thought her mind wrestled to comprehend and put to rest. *I don't know which is worse, here or the plantation. At least I had become accustomed to the plantation—a place where I knew every path. I return there in my sleep or when I feel unraveled, and I become whole and peaceful again.* Often when she woke up, she wouldn't know where she was. "Why didn't I run away?" she asked herself repeatedly.

If only I had Kuba to cling to, she thought. *I would face everything fearlessly.* But she reminded herself that he had run off to the hills in the prevailing madness of runaway slaves. So radical was the change in him it was as if someone else was thinking with his brain and looking out of his eyes—a man whose obsession was ridding the island of all planters.

On Saturday, after dinner, Robert called Penda from the kitchen. This had become her daily hangout. He thought she had been avoiding him. He outlined to her all the options he knew of in Lancashire for a single woman having a baby. He explained to her that an unmarried woman who became pregnant had limited choices, and for many, the only possible route was to give up their child to the Foundling Hospital. Their only hope of getting their child back was to find a respectable job as a servant. To get their child back, the woman would need to submit a written petition to prove she was of previous good character, then be forced to describe details of her sex life to a panel of middle-aged and elderly men.

Many of the women were illiterate, or unlike, Penda could read but could not write, having never been taught. Petitions would be written by someone else and submitted on their behalf. The women would have to collect a form from the porter's lodge at the hospital, where, unknown to them, the porter would make notes on things like appearance and attach it to their file. He knew that those mothers who were successful in getting the hospital to take their baby were pushed out of the picture and visiting was not encouraged. Hence, no relationship would or could be formed with the children. Servants were usually required to live in their employers' homes and were unable to have their children live with them.

"When a mother elects to hand over her baby, it is to avoid the scandal of raising a child born out of wedlock. No one here in Lancashire knows that you have a husband. The hospital will care for your child until it becomes a teenager, then they send it out into the world with a new name and a past made more acceptable in the hopes of never being stigmatized for the circumstances of its birth," he explained.

"What I have just told you is to help you make up your mind about the bairn."

Robert wished his mother was still alive as he was certain she would know what to do.

An uneasy silence settled over the two of them as Penda digested the enormity of caring for her child. For a long time, she remained sitting, feeling crushed and helpless. She let the silence linger for a while, thinking that, at that moment, silence was better than words. She chided herself for being so simple, for thinking life would be better anywhere but the plantation. She felt anger rising toward her husband, Kuba.

"What is the use of this anger," she asked herself, "when the only person who matters to me has refused to give up his pride, and now, I am faced with being alone?"

Perhaps she loved him, but her love was changing into something less confident, less trusting. It was becoming diseased with a pity that was close to contempt. Her loyalty to him was weakening as she struggled to steel herself to become a mother in an unknown world. Forgiveness forced its way into her heart, followed by relief, which enabled her to throw out of her thoughts, all doubts and distrust of Robert. And she firmly determined to give him no cause to regret saving her. She would work very hard around the house and try to appear contented as she was.

For Penda, that night was long and sleepless as she reviewed, compared, and contrasted the events of her time spent in England and the time spent on the plantation.

Thoughts of the sea and the idea of seeing Kuba occasionally remained close to her tempting her to indulge in the fantasy. Reality would make itself known soon enough, she thought. She forced herself to recite a verse from the Bible, but the moment her concentration wandered, she returned to Kuba on the plantation.

That night, Robert also spent some time reviewing his years spent in Jamaica. His initial plan was to take over his father's plantation after he died and return to England as soon as possible with the wealth he believed he could have amassed from sugar. He planned to buy Downham Manor and live like a gentleman. He knew nothing about planting sugarcane or the day-to-day running of a plantation of slaves. Initially, he was appalled at the treatment of human beings stripped of their common humanness. Now as a changed man, he found it difficult to think of this girl as a slave of Master Mapp or having his name branded on her body.

"They are all human," were the words spoken out loud to the empty barn the following morning. "And yes, they are people with names, and parents like me, homes, and identities I took away from them. The touch of a human hand, love, a hug, warmth—all these things are foreign to them." As a young man, he remembered wanting to be thought of as someone with status. As an only child, he was expected to follow his father as a slave owner. As a slave owner, he initially resolved to be different. On arriving in Jamaica, he found that his plans and resolutions changed. His mind in certain situations became undisturbed by acts or ideas of cruelty. They no longer seemed out of the ordinary, and instead, they seemed necessary. Now he had been profoundly transformed by a powerful experience of religious awakening. After such a life-changing experience, he wanted to end the trade in humans. He made a vow to his mother before she passed that he would do everything in his power to end it.

"Son, it is profitable, and trying to end it may become dangerous going against the men who have become rich from the trade."

"I'm a new man now as the Bible says, and old things are passed away. I don't want to compromise my principles." As he walked out of her room, he lifted his eyes to heaven and prayed for the strength to do it.

His thoughts returned to Catherine whom he planned to see the following morning before he went out to the farm.

He knew Catherine very well. Her mother's family was not from the landed gentry. On more than one occasion, she had expressed to him hatred of her father, blaming him for the snubs she sometimes imagined she received before her marriage to Matthew Mapp. Gossip had it that she had looked at Matthew with a speculative eye for a long time as it was known throughout the village that his grandfather had acquired his wealth from the sugarcane plantation he owned in Barbados. She had become increasingly bitter, being excluded from the tea parties, balls, and the social circle of the well-known Lady Scarborough, which was a symbol of refinement and identity to her.

He knew that women like Catherine did not marry for love, but instead, they tended to marry strictly for financial and social motives. A gentleman of high rank would not consider marrying a woman from a poor family because she would not possess the social graces and dowry required to marry into society. If they got married, rumors could be hatched that the match had only come about because he had gotten a girl "in the family way"—a situation that would become a humiliation to both him and his family name.

He knew that she was aware of what life would be like married to a man like Matthew. He of the landed gentry and she of a lower class was the motive behind accepting Matthew's proposal to marry and relocate to Barbados. The town knew that it was a marriage of convenience and that Catherine had no property or income for him to become entitled to as per British law, so marriage to a wealthy man had always been her object. She once confided in a mutual friend that it was the only honorable provision made for poor educated women, and being married made Matthew legally responsible for her support and protection.

Robert was familiar with the ruthlessness, resentment, and jealousies of the mistresses toward the slave girls who could give the planters a baby every year while the mistresses only in name slept alone most nights.

The memory of his history as a slave owner still percolated within his consciousness. It seemed like his memory survived despite the persistence of the Bible verses memorized that tried to suppress it. His inherited wealth and ascendancy in society he knew came from the plantations. Women like Penda were his property, and the slave codes introduced by his father and the island planters came from their fear of the slaves. Becoming a slave was not their choice, and childhood being a period of innocence did not exist on the plantation.

"I was foolish enough to go along with the belief that the more inhumane treatment experienced by the children the better prepared they would be for life." He felt overwhelmed by feelings of revulsion and shame—shame that he could practice such inhumane actions on another race and shame to stand and watch or look the other way.

There were sins of slavery he could not forget even though he had forgiven and received forgiveness. "What I have failed to see was the moral ruin of the system." Planters became cruel, and their children followed suit. Wives are miserable and forced to turn a blind eye to the acts of their husbands. Conversations would be of poor ruined crops, a bad harvest from scanty rainfall, or other conditions but not of the environment that ruined the lives of human beings.

Here in England, many young women in domestic service were severely punished by the law for giving birth to illegitimate babies.

Robert was aware that African-trained domestic servants could be sold and bought as they were of indeterminate status. He wanted the girl to know that they were both made in God's image, that she should never describe herself as a slave of no man, that she was created not something that just happened. Even in this oppressive and what seems unfair life, he wanted her to know she could choose hope or give in to despair and engage in praise and thankfulness instead of grumbling—so much he wanted to teach her. But it had to wait until Catherine Mapp made her decision.

Events followed each other in rapid succession in the few days, following Robert's decision to see Catherine. He deliberately delayed meeting with her as he knew the system and the difficulty of mistresses giving up black servants with official papers.

As promised, he went on Saturday morning around ten o'clock. It was completely unexpected. Nothing could have been further from her mind than this visit, and her first instinct on opening the door was to refuse entry.

"Good morning, Robert. What brings you here?" Catherine said with a smirk.

With her hand still on the door, after a few minutes, she beckoned him in, turned, and walked into the parlor. She took a deep breath and repeated her question.

As self-predicted, her attitude was very cordial.

"Tea for the gentleman?"

"Yes, thank you. That would be lovely," Robert responded with the same false cheerfulness.

"I am very impressed by how well you look and your influence in the community," Catherine mocked.

He looked at her in silence for a few seconds, then he settled his back against the chair offered.

"I know you moved away from here when you got married to Matthew Mapp. Are you back for good now?"

Catherine got up and walked to the window, and there she stood for what seemed like a long while.

"I came back after my husband's death for two reasons: Matthew left me nothing but debts he accrued over a bad business deal that went wrong, and I hope as I'm still young, I may be able to marry again and have children." She deliberately left out the money he noted.

"How long has it been since he died Catherine?"

"Four years ago, he passed away—" Catherine stopped speaking and wiped tears that were streaming down her cheeks.

"I trust you are fully recovered from your husband's untimely death. These must be very hard days for you since he left you so ill-provided for and, on top of that, burdened you with his unpaid debts. I hope that his family can help you financially."

In Catherine's eyes, she was ready to be married since she had mourned her husband at the socially accepted time.

What she did not tell him was that she scarcely grieved when her husband died, and in her lucid moments, she saw the many possibilities of gaining wealth from sugar as a merchant's wife, as well as definite standing in the elite social circles through being married to one of the landed gentries. It was pure luck that she had married Matthew, but he had let every penny from sugar slip through his fingers.

"One good thing that came out of Barbados was one of the slaves I brought back from the island as my personal servant. She served me very well there when I became sick."

"I'm here to talk to you about her, Sarah, as you know her."

"Why?"

As Robert sat with Catherine on his first visit, there were some uncomfortably long periods of silence; both were lost in their thoughts. He thought of the risks he was running as an abolitionist, but Penda's situation presented him with an opportunity to keep fighting for the freedom of slaves. He pondered his choice and the decision of her husband to run after the stories of money to be found in sugar on plantations of the Caribbean. After having a radical life change, Robert realized the money gotten by unscrupulous means could not and did not buy her husband or his father one day longer of life, neither could it bribe death. They all got the same notice since the length of days was decided by God alone.

The standards that the planters set for themselves and for the slaves were not the same. He wished he had done things differently, but it was too late now, and he couldn't walk back to the past.

"My housekeeper informs me that you threw her out of your house because she is with child by your husband. Is that true?

"Oh no, I thought that at first, but after I threw her out, I thought differently. The father of her baby may be a runaway slave."

"If that is the case, why throw her out with no money and nowhere to stay?"

"I cannot afford for her to have her baby and live here as people who don't know that Matthew is dead will believe that—"

"She has been staying at the farm, helping my housekeeper Mrs. Beckett. Should I turn her out as well?" he asked.

"Yes, do you know what people are saying about her and you in the village?"

"No, tell me."

"They are saying that something funny is going on at your house. You have always been such a well-respected man and your father before you. I don't think you should live with a young slave girl like that, Robert".

"I don't want to hear gossip. It is one of this village's few entertainments." He thought of the days when a village community was closely knit. When the villagers rarely went further than their own market town, people knew a great deal about each other and were always eager to learn more.

"There is no smoke without fire."

"Where am I to send her?" Robert asked quietly.

"That's not your problem."

"Well," Robert said, "the girl is no problem. We shall have to think of something. How much did you pay for her in Barbados?"

"Nothing, I was giving her food and a place to sleep in a house as opposed to a mud hut." Robert knew she was not telling the truth; she or her husband must have paid the trader an amount.

Having won her point, she seemed anxious to placate him and began to talk about other things. It seemed true that there were comments made about the black servant at Downham Farm and that most people were prepared to believe the worst, adding their opinions.

"I would like to offer her employment at the farm if you have no objection, and seeing you brought her to England and can't afford to keep her."

"Let me think about your proposal, Robert. I will give you an answer in one week." The agreement was made on a day for the following week. Catherine had succeeded in seeing him once more.

Of course, he would have liked a decision, seeing through Catherine's attempt to deal with her loneliness and need for a man, one with affluence and money.

As he drove home in his buggy, he reflected on how fashionable it had become in English society to have a black servant. Before Robert went to Jamaica, he was repelled by the idea that human beings could be bought and sold like sugar and rum. He had tried to put slavery out of his mind until he met Penda. Now seeing her daily brought everything back. That people like the girl could be taken against their will and owned body and soul by people who looked like him and his father before he made him turn away. He bowed his head and prayed for wisdom and God's intervention in the situation and for favor with Catherine.

For the whole week, following Robert's visit to Catherine, he was silent, grim-faced, and unapproachable. Penda got worried, having never seen him like this during the three weeks she was his housekeeper. He seemed subdued.

Had something happened at Mistress's house that was responsible for this silence? she asked herself.

Robert made no comment to Penda about his visit to Mistress Catherine. His attitude remained the same, and he didn't seem to be aware that she was living on a razor's edge. He kept up his routine on the farm. The reason for this was that he knew Penda did not always understand what he said. But she showed a readiness to learn, and he enjoyed using her native intelligence, which was divorced from the racial, cultural, and educational factors that she was exposed to on the plantation.

He reviewed the conversation with Catherine many times during the week. He didn't like the disparaging remarks made about the slaves, including Penda. He had tried unsuccessfully to stop her by explaining that these slaves were made in God's image like her. However, he believed that ending on bad terms with her could place Penda in a position to be sent back to Barbados since she was still powerful in name as a Mapp. What Robert believed when he studied her was he saw a woman whose morals and mind were as muddled as his while a planter in the Caribbean.

The pain and destruction he caused for a few pounds could not keep his father or mother alive. "The past cannot be remade," he chided himself, "but the future can. It's a fool's game to try to predict what would have happened if…"

He thought of Penda. He thought her beautiful. Her face had filled in the weeks she had stayed at the farm. In another world, he could love her if not married, but she was married. The last conversation with his father was heated. He had given his dad an account of the things he had done on the plantation, his disgust at himself sleeping with any slave he chose—married or single.

He recalled an incident where the woman's husband walked in from the field, catching him in a compromised position. He could never forget the look on the man's face as he turned and walked out of the hut. While he got dressed as he walked out, the man's head remained down. He was conscious only of revulsion and shame, shame that he and his father practiced such atrocities.

When he finally came to his senses, he admitted to himself he was no better than the plantation owners he knew. He who caused the suffering to make themselves rich by the world's standards. Robert's heart change came after reading his father's Bible. He learned his father and the preacher were wrong when they preached there was no equality. At the time, he felt foolish. The story his father told him was that sugar had rescued his family from bankruptcy and poverty.

The Sunday following Robert's visit to Catherine, he came home for lunch. Penda was at the sink, washing dishes and cleaning up the kitchen. He greeted Penda, then went to the back door, and looked out.

"Do you miss the church services on the plantation?" he asked. It was now some weeks since he had encountered the girl. She didn't want to think about anything to do with God. After all the shame of being thrown out, she couldn't believe that God cared about her.

"No, 'cause Mammy and my friend gone," Penda answered as a tear escaped. What Penda missed was the routines and the people. Adjusting to a new way of life was difficult, she admitted.

"If Penda is your Christian name, what is your family name?" Penda didn't know why he was questioning her on this matter.

"I don't have other name," she said.

"Well, you need a family name. Mine is Parker. What was the name of your tribe? Can you remember the name of your village?"

"Lunda village, and my tribe is Karembe."

"Why don't you take part of the name of your tribe like Kare? Then you would be Penda Kare. It's easy to spell, and the baby you are carrying when born would have a family name and could be registered easily." Penda thought about his suggestion for a minute but remained silent. When a response from Penda was not forthcoming, Robert advised her to think about it and left for the farm. *How jittery she is this morning*, Robert thought. *And now I have made her more so by asking her questions about her name and tribe.*

At Catherine's house, there was a housekeeper and a gardener. The housekeeper, Mrs. Heatherington, was an older woman, Penda thought, judging from the gray hair peeking out from her bonnet. She had been housekeeper to Catherine's brother and sister-in-law. She moved slowly when climbing the stairs with trays but expressed her thanks to Catherine for some help in the kitchen. For three days, the housekeeper gave Penda instructions on how to scrub vegetables and wash and dry plates and silverware. There were days when the girl ate leftovers from Catherine's table to stave off the hunger that gnawed on the inside.

On the Sunday of her third week, the housekeeper announced to Penda, "Mistress wants me to teach you today how to make her tea. This way, if I'm not here, you will have no difficulty. Warm the teapot with hot water from a saucepan." All the time, she complained about the demands Catherine made on her at any hour of the day or night. "Be sure to put the tea leaves in the teapot before adding the water, and the milk must be boiling and the cream fresh," she added as an afterthought.

"Ma'am, I don't know what tea leaves look like." She glared at Penda with a disdainful look. Mrs. Heatherington was never a slave and, for a moment, had forgotten that she had taught the girl how to cook simple foods like mashed potatoes, roast beef, and gravy.

As an abolitionist, Robert's meetings with other abolitionists were not announced. They were fighting to abolish slave codes that said slaves should not be taught to read or helped to escape. They spoke out against slavery.

It was a Monday morning, about eight o'clock, seven sunsets after she arrived in England. Penda was called to the library. "I have a list of goods I need you to get from the village shops, and here is the money," Mistress ordered.

"Yes, Ma'am." Penda looked at the list, thankful she had been taught to read, but there were words she had never seen before like bacon, scone, pound, tomato, shop, and shillings—not words in the Bible, her main reference—and she did not know the correct pronunciation of them.

When she closed the gate, she felt strange, and her legs felt a bit wobbly. This would be her first time going out of the house since her arrival. She looked at her clothes and thought of how conspicuous she would look among a sea of white faces. The weather was cold, with a fine drizzle, and the sun was breaking through the mist. She followed the instructions as they were written. She turned right down the first street, then left, and left again, then across a square—there was a row of shops. She had to be careful where she put her feet to avoid horse droppings. The fruit and vegetable stalls were a mass of colors, oranges, tomatoes, lemons, and purple vegetables.

"What be name of these?" she asked the woman at the stall.

"They are aubergines."

And to some shiny round, red and yellow vegetables, the inquiring look on Penda's face brought a response from the woman.

"Peppers. Where do you come from that you don't know them?" she asked.

"No, ma'am. They are not on my list." The woman shook her head as the girl moved on to stalls selling herbs like parsley and thyme.

Moving next to the fish stall, she was a complete novice as she had never seen herring, cod, smoked mackerel, or smoked salmon. She knew flying fish as they were plentiful in Barbados.

The last shop she entered was the butchers. She had become familiar with the words used by the housekeeper like mutton, roast beef, fowl, potatoes, and cabbage.

"What do you say, gal?" Penda was quiet. "Speak up," the man wearing a blood-stained white coat said. *He is addressing me, expecting a reply*, she thought.

"One pound of lamb, please." Penda had practiced and rehearsed the list on the walk.

"That would be ten shillings."

Having not been taught money on the plantation or in England, the girl did not know what to do. She placed all her money on the counter while trying to explain she didn't speak the language and didn't understand. After a while, the butcher shrugged, took what was his due, and resumed cutting the meat. She put the change and the meat in her bag, thinking how funny it was carrying a bag with groceries. She did that each week until she learned to recognize and count money.

Having been confined to the house for a week, there were unfamiliar sights and words of her new world she was forced to grasp like pavement, buildings stuck together called houses, a street full of shops in a row that sold everything from buttons to vegetables. Greengrocers and butchers were called a parade. She learned that there were people living above the shops. There were foods like fish and chips, porridge, or a contraption called a hoover that sucked up dirt from the carpet. Each morning, she was awakened by a faceless voice coming from a box called a radio and distant sounds called ringing bells coming from a place called a church.

She learned about the best potatoes for roasting and how to queue up, the importance of a cup of tea in England, the discovery of a bathtub and its function, the sound of the milkman, and the word *hawker* meaning a seller.

Penda did not know about the months of the year or how to count them by name. There was a book in the kitchen called a calendar from which she was taught by the housekeeper.

Sterling pounds, shillings, and pence were the basic currency of England. Twelve pence equaled one shilling and twenty shillings equaled one sterling pound.

No one had prepared her for this new world.

At the grocer, she read prices: tea, half a pound, one shilling. Thankful she could read, Penda continued to review the displayed list: bread, loaf, 1 shilling, 2 pence; butter, 1 shilling; milk, 1 bottle, 10 pence; sugar, 4 pounds, 10 pence; vegetables, 4 pence; sausages and pies, 4 shillings.

Shopping at the butcher was to be done daily. It was the only place one could buy meat and sausages because of the lack of refrigeration.

The list was divided into two headings: breakfast and dinner.

Under breakfast items were bread, margarine, eggs, and jam while under dinner were one pound of lamb and one pound of potatoes.

There were things Penda had to learn quickly like the people's status in society by their dress or people with dogs on leashes, the clatter of horses' hooves, and the crack of a coachman's whip. There was a clock that chimed on the hour that helped teach her time. She had never seen paper on walls from ceiling to the floor or eating utensils that had to be polished and a tabletop in which one could see their face. Plates and drinking cups were given the name China.

The tasks assigned by Catherine were stripping sheets, scrubbing floors, fastening the back of the mistress's corset, emptying the urine pot, washing China plates and spoons, dusting tables and desks, helping Mrs. Heatherington with the laundry and ironing, serving cups of tea, and helping Catherine bathe in water Penda hauled and warmed. Penda worked so hard, doing everything mistress set out for her to do, that most nights when she tumbled in her bed at eleven o'clock, sleep came immediately.

Every day Penda walked to the shops, she believed people stared as there were no black faces seen in the shops or in the village where she did Catherine's shopping. Some of the people she passed on the street would follow her with their eyes.

She was used to the warmth of hot weather, fresh sea water for her baths, and early morning ventures to the sea in Barbados had become one daily pleasure and a sense of freedom.

Chigwell the town had a single road running through the center with grass at one end, a building called a church, and another building called a school. Then there were puzzling aspects to the complexities of the English language with its subtle distinctions and pronunciations; everything about England was unfamiliar. As a servant, she had to learn about the British currency—the pound, shillings, and pence—how to count it and how to spend it. She lacked social skills like how to communicate in proper English. Then there was the social etiquette she had to learn like how to walk on cobbled streets without getting run over or looking in the mistress's face when receiving instructions, how to communicate with other servants she would meet in the market, and how to sit and stand gracefully as following social rules was very important for personal servants. There were other rules taught by the housekeeper on her first day.

On discovering the library, she began sneaking books to her room where she kept them under her bed. She knew she shouldn't, but at every chance, she visited the library and stood in front of the shelves while casting glances at the door and listening for the sound of footsteps that would betray her presence.

She must have fallen into a deep sleep. The boy looked to be seven years old, she was sure of that. Five years was the age for children to be either sold or sent to the field. While the cook rambled on about the gossip of the plantation, Penda turned her attention to the small, serious child hidden in the corner of the kitchen playing with sticks.

Penda turned away to the child in the farthest corner of the kitchen as it was away from the eyes of anyone coming through the door like the overseer.

"Whats your name?" she asked the child.

"Nmadi, but massuh say Solomon."

Penda picked up the boy and tickled him till he relaxed, giggled, and finally burst into uncontrollable laughter. Through the boy, she saw the emptiness of her village with only old women left behind. She told the boy about her village, her brother, but was not sure if he understood. Then she wept over the thought that this boy would be sold soon.

Penda was torn from her sleep by a loud knocking on the bedroom door. Her eyes opened into darkness. Startled, her brain quickly registered her whereabouts as Downham Farm.

"Are you having pain?" a man's voice shouted.

"No, suh, me not in pain, be dreaming."

"Must have been a very bad dream for such loud weeping."

Penda remained on the bed in darkness while her thoughts returned to the boy and his childhood. She imagined the loneliness and bewilderment of Nmadi finding himself sold to different plantations many times before reaching manhood.

Her thoughts remained on the dream and the uncertainty of her future for a long time. In the dark, she prayed and questioned how in her situation she would be able to train up her child in the way it should go as the Bible instructs. She gave thanks to God for arranging her meeting with Robert. Without his help, she thought she might not have survived.

The *Chronicle* newspaper was delivered three times a week to Chigwell Manor. Penda routinely read the advertisements for runaway servants to be returned to their houses of employment and masters or mistresses. Each week, her reading brought the same response—a shudder, a sick feeling of fear and anxiety as she contemplated her precarious position and that of her unborn baby of possibly being returned to slavery.

As she lay there, she made several attempts to reconstruct the last days at Catherine before she was thrown out. After repeated failures, she began a mental diary, putting together pieces of conversation, little events that may have highlighted Catherine as a not-so-nice person.

"You will start at six o'clock in the morning."

"Yes, ma'am, but me don't know what six o'clock mean," Penda answered.

"That is a time," she said sharply. "Do you not hear the chimes of a clock?"

"Yes, ma'am, me hear sometime."

"Every hour strikes according to the time. Can you count?"

Penda nodded, trying to hide her confusion and responded, "Yes, ma'am, up to ten."

"Well, you will have to learn. Your tasks are to be done by the clock," she tried to explain. Penda did her best to follow Mistress Mapp's complicated instructions. She understood she needed to count time with the clock.

"When the clock strikes six times in the morning, you are to be downstairs in the kitchen with the housekeeper."

"Yes, mistress." Penda remained standing until Catherine turned and walked upstairs. That night, she slept fitfully listening to the clock chimes.

CHAPTER 2

The big house, the cries of the birds, the shrill of crickets—she missed them, as well as the sea. All reminded her of the plantation.

Here in England, no one cares who I am, she acknowledged. *I'm beginning from zero again, being thrown out with a baby and nowhere to live. The past never left me, instead, it has returned in vivid color.* She was slowly becoming acquainted with the culture and customs of the British by, first, concentrating on the basic language of English. She remembered straining to understand what her mistress was saying, but eventually before leaving the island, she could carry on a limited conversation with her. She remembered when she finally succeeded at reading how suddenly the strange black twists and turns on the pages of the bible were assembled into a word.

Now, after a little over six months in Lancashire, I am beginning to see it as my home and an avenue of freedom. The transition to freedom is terrifying, having spent all my teen years in slavery or servitude. I never had decisions to make about my life. Everything was decided for me—when to get up in the morning; when to start my day, eat, and sleep; and when to do say, live, and serve God exactly as the preacher and planters said. Now I face freedom and responsibility. Now I am being asked to make decisions for myself and my unborn baby.

Reflections of motherhood on the plantation and keeping one's children depended on the whims of the master or the finances or size of the debt. What good then is having children, enjoying them for a few minutes or a few months before they are sold? And you, the mother and father, never see them again or what it is like not to see your children grow up with you? It must be very painful, she thought.

Penda was never exposed to anything that a normal person experienced when transitioning from youth to adulthood. Being in England, she realized she was free, but there was still so much to learn—how to cook and how to make friends. She lacked social skills like how to communicate in proper English. She had to learn how to look in her mistress's face when receiving instructions and how to stand still gracefully and keep her hands behind her back when speaking to the mistress; never call from one room to another were instilled by the housekeeper on her first day.

For the present, however, Penda thought she had enough to do to learn how to be a housekeeper and prepare for the birth of her baby.

In a way, though free, she found it difficult to leave the plantation on the inside because the plantation was all she knew, and the memories she could salvage of life in the village were fading.

Being recaptured and sold was always present, but the acuity of the pain of loss had mellowed. Many of her questions started with *why*. To Penda, it seemed like whatever privileges she may have gained working for Catherine could be taken away in a flash. To Penda, it meant that the absence of her past and a doubtful future were the places from which God chose for her to grow, but it made her vulnerable.

There are no answers to my questions, she told herself. *Yet I am unable to turn off or silence the voices in my head that need answers.* Eventually, she reached a temporary conclusion that the answers were beyond her human understanding. It was settled. This was a new start—an opportunity for forgiveness to care and to be treated as a human. The plantation had removed what the term *human* was meant to encompass the freedom to be vulnerable.

At times, when Penda felt isolated and friendless, despondency overruled her. She scarcely noticed the passage of days through the first two months of her time in England, those days remaining in her memory as a blur. And yet as depressed, lonely, despondent, and friendless as she was, she didn't give up entirely. She believed that every experience had an end if only she could hang on long enough to see it.

By the close of June, when she had been at Downham Manor for about six weeks, things had improved enough, providing nourishment for her will and helping her submerging heart to begin to rise in hope.

"I think to myself now, God will make a way, and I have faith that he will not forsake me." There was a knowing that she had not escaped the horrors of the plantation to be like an appendage without purpose. "I know now that I have a purpose in life, but what is it, Lord? Because if I don't know it, my life would be empty."

As she washed her face the following morning, she felt that a new life was beginning for her and in her, but she predicted that it would be a new life without her husband, Kuba.

"What is your name?" This question asked by Master Parker repeated itself often at night. The name she spontaneously gave him "Sarah, slave of Master Mapp" had become her identity. She remembered initially making a promise to never forget the name Penda, but that became a challenge for her memory to keep the two names ready for recall.

She understood the word *slave* or *servant* applied to her meant that she was expected and obligated to perform a defined set of actions, behaviors, and routines on the plantation and in England. In Barbados, it meant she was expected to be up before dawn and work all day, stopping only when allowed usually after sunset. If there was light, she was expected to work.

The identity of a *slave* was permanent even to her offspring, perpetually a reality that Penda had never really stopped evaluating. She realized that even after she had adopted all the customs, beliefs, and attitudes that were characteristic of slaves, it was still not her ethnic identity.

She recognized her powerlessness to change those features that people saw of her that were out of her choosing. She wanted to be able to choose, yet even here in England, her decisions were weighed by someone else.

Sold and *bought* were the two words whose meaning she understood—words that sealed her identity as a piece of property to be gotten rid of or bought in exchange for money.

It was a Monday evening in early autumn; the weather was nice for taking a walk. Penda left the house for a quick walk to the farm and back. She collected a basket of eggs and walked back to the house. As she approached the house, she was about to go in by the back when she noticed the back door was open and voices were heard coming from the kitchen. Instinctively, she paused, not wanting to disturb Mr. Parker and his guest. She thought of walking in the garden until he had finished. But while she weighed her thoughts on what action to take, she heard the familiar voice of his housekeeper, Mrs. Beckett, who seemed angry.

"I'm not saying that you should or should not marry Catherine Mapp, but you, now being a changed man, need to treat the girl as your Bible instructs…as you treat yourself. I believe that Catherine will ill-treat her and the baby if the girl is sent back. That would be cruel."

"What am I to do with the girl?" Robert asked in a pleading tone. "She's with child." Mr. Parker's voice sounded tired.

His mind went back to when he found her. It was true that she had been thrown out of somewhere, but he never foresaw this dilemma.

"Why don't you just keep her and offer Mrs. Mapp some money for her? As a wealthy landowner in your forties, you could secure a good wife."

"I'm not ready to commit to family life yet, and to your first suggestion, I can't pay money for Penda because you know that, by law, I need Catherine's permission and the girl's free papers."

"Alright," he assured her, "I'll do something about it. Don't worry Mrs. Beckett. The girl is fine, and you know I have been a changed man since my mother died."

"Since you are a changed man, you know what the Bible commands us to do toward one another. I worry about you being an only child as you have no children to inherit your legacy when you are gone."

"I will go see Catherine tomorrow" were the last words Penda heard.

Penda did not wait to hear anymore. She stumbled away on the grass so that she would not be discovered eavesdropping and began walking back in the direction she came. Out of sight of the house, she stopped, unable to go on. She leaned against a fence post with her heart heavy inside of her.

Acute disappointment flooded into her. She had hoped Mr. Parker was able to settle everything for her. Yes, she had to face it—she was not important to him. He was just doing her kindness.

In the kitchen, Robert was facing Mrs. Beckett.

"No need to reproach yourself," Mrs. Beckett said. "I'm fully aware that you were doing what you thought was your duty."

"On the subject of marriage, you can be quite sure that I wouldn't be entering into a marriage I don't want. I'm not ready to commit to family life yet. The woman I choose to marry will be God-fearing and have similar values, temperament, and intelligence. I would not let gossip or public opinion hound me into doing anything I object to."

"Well, I had to come and see for myself."

That night, Mrs. Beckett's words played repeatedly in Robert's head through a sleepless night. He regretted what he did as a planter in Jamaica. He knew it wouldn't bring back his parents or remove the pain and destruction he caused for a few pounds. He counseled himself with the thought that his past could not be remade but his future could. If things happened as the young woman related, then it wasn't difficult to see the picture of her mistress being a mentally sick woman.

The next day, he went to see Catherine with a plan.

Penda wished she had not heard the conversation because what she heard dropped something heavy on her heart that reinforced the precarious nature of her status. However, what she hoped for was to be employed as a housekeeper to Mr. Parker and to be free to raise her child. Penda was not seeking to acquire anything beyond a subsistence for herself and her child. She reasoned that if he married Catherine, she may still be sent away. This important but desolating possibility took all her joy away as well, along with the anticipation of being his housekeeper and possibly being taught to write.

She watched Parker and his housekeeper get up to leave, and to avoid meeting them, she turned back and walked around the house to the other side. There she waited until she heard the buggy leave, then entered the kitchen with a sinking heart. She made sure they were gone, then she leaned back on the chair, trying to block out what she had heard, afraid to make predictions on the possible outcomes of the conversation. She was left with the problem of what she would do if Parker decided to let her go.

In the weeks before being thrown out in the streets, Catherine seemed to be on the verge of regressing to a state of insanity again. Whenever she became uncontrollably hysterical, Penda would express concern, and she would seem to pull herself together. She started sleeping for long periods, and when awake, she would stare without focus. Sometimes in her lucid moments, she would pray or ask Penda to pray for her. As these bouts increased, Penda's trust in Catherine and the promises she made to her in Barbados decreased. "I will take good care of you and teach you to read and write." What Penda knew was that Catherine could sell her to Barbados or anywhere that needed slaves.

So daily fear-inducing words like "what if" would visit at times, crippling her; what if Master Robert had left her in the thunderstorm or had tricked her and planned to sell her into slavery again? However, against the fear and in the privacy of her thoughts, some of Mammie's last words would come to her: "The day will come when you are free." Such fears were not totally unfounded as she often read in the weekly reports of the *Chronicle* newspaper about small shipments of runaway West Indian servants being sent to Barbados without any explanation.

"Lord, I am not something that just happened, so even in this situation, I am choosing to hope and be thankful to you for using Catherine to take me away from the plantation. This Bible says you are God who is always awake, then surely now you must be aware of my situation."

Taking each day as it came, Penda reassured herself that she and the baby would survive.

In England, life was certainly better: She thought of the food she had access to and she was happy learning to cook English food (simply potatoes every which way with beef from the butchers a practice or skill she was never exposed to). In her personal contentment, Penda was slowly becoming less conscious of the sufferings of the slaves left behind or at least was less disturbed by them. Even so, two things weighed heavily on her mind: one was separation from Kuba, and the other was what was going to happen to her baby as a final decision had not been made by Robert and Catherine.

Robert also remained quiet on the visit to Mistress, thus keeping an air of suspense hanging over their head, knowing that her place as a servant would prohibit her from speaking unless spoken to or asking any questions.

Feelings of fear and anguish previously experienced before now overwhelmed her, shattering the feeling of hope she had brought to England. What was certain was the instability of a home and a relationship. In response to the bits of the conversation overheard, she shook her head in helpless frustration and prayed as Mammy's voice came: "Penda, you have it in you to go forward. No use fretting over the past or the future. God will keep you safe as he has done already."

"Becoming a slave or, in this case, a servant was not by my choice, Lord." This concluded with hesitation that there was one who knew what was best for her, and this someone had a great design for her life because he promised in the Bible to order her steps. She prayed as she prepared supper.

"Lord, I cannot see the ending right now, but I know that where there is a beginning there must be an ending. I cannot go back, I can only go forward one step at a time with your help until I come to the end."

Maybe, she argued silently that God had nothing to do with her enslavement or her presence in England, that it just happened. But then, it would be easier to endure the uncertainty of this situation if she knew for sure that he had nothing to do with it. She wanted to believe her ancestors that life and death just happened.

"Where can I go?" she asked out loud. "At least in Barbados, I knew where I was, and I had some form of fragile attachment to the other slaves. At this moment, I feel it matters little where I go or what becomes of me. I am disheartened and disappointed in Catherine and without the ability to choose." Penda was using words she had read in the many books of Catherine, hoping they made sense.

For the first six months, Penda was happy to be living in England, away from the sounds of the plantation. And so she allowed herself to think about the freedom to weigh carefully what it would be like to make her own rules instead of following the plans of a master or mistress. She was alive and, one day, would tell her story of survival to her child.

When Robert returned from his second visit to Catherine, he gave no sign that he had even discussed her. She felt disappointed. On the second visit, as the subject of Penda was introduced, Catherine reminded him that the feelings of the servant were secondary and beneath consideration. Robert thought she looked more relaxed today, dressed in a soft gray dress, her hair loose around her face. She showed him to one couch, and she sat opposite, facing him and the window. Without looking at him, she said, "Alright, you wish me to come to some arrangement about Sarah?"

"Yes. But her name is Penda." She looked at him for a while, then she glanced occasionally at the garden where a man was pruning a bush or shrub.

"I would have thought that, since you do not want her here granting me, all her papers would be easy," Robert said, a bit irritated.

"How much money are you offering?" Catherine asked, punctuating her question with a distracting cough that he was beginning to think, maybe, a conversational habit. Her involuntary throat clearing was also something he missed on his first visit.

"If we could agree on a sum." A little cough again, clearing of the throat, and a girlish toss of the hair—another glance at the garden, a pursing of her lips. She walked to the window, threw it open, and called to the man to leave the shrub. "It's the wrong season for that," she muttered to herself and returned to the proposition.

"Is three hundred pounds suitable?" Robert asked. He wished he had found a different way to phrase the question since he had no thought of treating Penda like a piece of property. Catherine went silent, held her hands still, looked at Robert for a second, then looked out the window. He thought that something had been miscommunicated, causing him to fear achieving a settlement that day. Even friendliness was not possible. He thought she displayed disinterest in the girl's welfare and that of her unborn child. Aside from her coldness, Robert was beginning to think of Catherine exactly as the person Penda described to him—an insane woman.

She was obviously angry. Anger and hatred burned in her words.

"Have you discovered something bad about the girl?" Robert asked. Catherine remained silent for a while.

"I am aware of the relation my husband had with some women on the plantation, a common occurrence among planters."

He had no response to that. Catherine was never a mother, and he sensed jealousy and envy.

Robert felt strange thinking of Catherine as a Mapp and not by her family name Thornton. As he thought of her name, *thornbush* was the image that appeared. She was a thornbush, he concluded. He tried to return to the questions he had prepared.

"What is your response to my suggestion?"

"You mean, why don't I sell her?"

"Yes, along with her freedom papers."

"I can't see that working."

"What about freeing her?" he finally asked.

"Yes, I suppose I could but not today. Let's arrange to have that done for you."

At that point, her housekeeper tapped on the door and entered with a tray of tea and biscuits. She placed it on the table and left, closing the door.

"Don't you want to ask me about Barbados?" she asked, chewing slowly. He was beginning to think she was either buying time or his visit was a pretense at conversation.

At the end of their visit, as Catherine was seeing him at the door, she confessed to Robert that the principles she thought she had while in England had become entangled and compromised in the plantation system.

"When did they change?" he asked.

She wasn't sure when. "I think I'm too tired to continue this visit today, but you are welcome to call on me tomorrow at the same time."

"Not tomorrow, maybe next week." As he closed her gate, walking to his buggy, he saw Catherine as someone unwilling to give up the power she held over the girl. The hope of making Penda a free woman died. He had calculated wrong. He had deliberated that she would have been glad to get rid of Penda and that she would have settled for anything. He also sensed she may have been hard-pressed for money, a problem he thought in his mind he could resolve. He was determined to get Penda's freedom at any cost.

When Parker left, Catherine thought she could get a higher price for the girl. She would not accept his first offer, but after reviewing all aspects of his offer, she concluded that she had better take it. "Where are the papers? Did I ever have them?" she asked herself, becoming frantic.

Penda was disappointed at not being told about the visit to Catherine. She began to weep as she cleaned the kitchen. She wept for the man she loved. She wept for the life they would not have together, for the things for which she could no longer dream. She wept in fear for Kuba. Would he be recaptured or beaten? Feeling dejected, she sat in a chair, closed her eyes, and must have slept until she was startled awake by the baby kicking in her tummy.

"Was I dreaming?" she asked herself.

Penda sat motionless, the memory bringing back to her mind all the events of her wedding night. There was no question of leaving the plantation, and she did not expect to leave.

Coming down the stairs, it was dark, but for a candle, Parker had left in the kitchen. He must have come home early and left her to sleep. Since coming to his house, she saw him only at mealtimes. What she did not know but discovered later was that he met with abolitionists who believed like him that slavery was wrong and were working on its abolishment. The slaves he bought were sent to Lady Avonlea's house, where they were taught to read, speak good English, and be good housekeepers. Metal collars with names engraved, he had them all removed.

It was when Penda and Mrs. Beckett were preparing cherries for bottling and jam that she learned a lot about Parker and his family.

"This is the best crop of cherries I have had in all the years I have worked for Robert and his family," the housekeeper announced as she walked in.

"A long time?" Penda asked.

"More than twenty years," Mrs. Beckett reckoned. "Mr. Parker—Master Robert, I called him—his mother had a pet name for him. He was a boy of nine or ten when I was brought here as a servant. He was as nice a lad as you would meet. Sorry, he was the only one. Mrs. Parker had two more children—both boys and both died a few days after they were born. She was very sick after the second child died, and that is when I was brought to help her."

"And how long since she died?"

"Four years this coming July, she passed."

Mrs. Beckett stopped speaking and wiped away the tears that were running down her cheeks.

Then she looked at the slim girl wrapped in her big apron, and her heart felt sadness for her. What would her future look like?

Penda went with Mrs. Beckett, Robert's housekeeper, one day to the market. They entered the grocery shop that served the wealthy, titled, and prosperous farmers. It was the only shop with wood counters, she noticed. The many times when she had gone shopping for Catherine, she had never entered Mr. Hart's shop. She always dealt with the smaller shops. Mr. Hart met them with a smile, then offered small bits of different cheeses until the housekeeper was satisfied and bought some. He advised the housekeeper about blends of tea and even sent her back with a sample of a blend.

"He does this every week until Robert finds one to his taste," she told Penda as they left. Until that market day, Penda had never noticed that the stalls all ran down one side of the street and offered everything from fish caught at the coast and fruit picked, from local orchards to boots and shoes, ribbons, trimmings, and all the threads for sewing and embroidery.

CHAPTER 3

One day in the spring, Penda was cleaning a room containing only books and papers. It was large with shelves. She knew that permission had not been given to be there, but she had discovered it, and at every chance, she would stand there with ogling eyes and guilty glances at the door. She would choose one book, slip it under the bed, and read when the house got quiet.

Robert made frequent trips to Bristol or London to attend abolitionist meetings. One of those days, when Robert was in Bristol, Penda and the housekeeper were alone in the house. Penda thought it would be a good day to clean the library—so many books to dust. There was a pile of unopened letters on the desk. On this day, it was her fortune to make a discovery. She was becoming familiar with his personal items like mail since Robert had become lax with organizing his personal things around the farm. She decided to leave the table for last. She was about to leave when she noticed what looked like a folded piece of cardboard, which, on examining closer, turned out to be a folder. When Penda picked up the folder, a thrill of excitement ran down her body. Something about it told her with certainty that the folder was of importance to her, yet that something contained a fleeting apprehension, an instinctive curiosity, that made her open it. Inside was a handwritten list of names of servants to be employed in Bristol. There was a price next to each name. She read the list eagerly. She was closing the folder when her eye caught a name at the end of the list, followed by a description: Absalom; 50 pounds; twenty-year-old male; healthy a fighter; great value; tall, strong; seems whole but for a brand on his back. She held the folder to her breast; the name connected her to the plantation.

"Lord," she prayed as her knees got weak. That was Kuba's name in Barbados. "Is this Kuba?" she asked herself. "Could this be real?" She looked at the list and touched it to assure herself she had seen his name. The floor seemed to be moving under her feet. She ran out the door to her room. In the days following, Penda longed to discuss her find with Parker but was afraid to reveal she was in his library.

On the third meeting with Catherine, she gave Robert a subservient smile and attempted superficial cordial conversation. He tried to be calm as he discussed Penda's future. He learned from the housekeeper that Penda's time to give birth was fast approaching. His housekeeper had helped her daughter deliver five babies. He learned from her housekeeper that she did not have the free papers as she pretended. He knew time was short but didn't want to appear anxious.

"For me to take her back, she would have to give her baby to the Foundling Hospital," Catherine stated with an attitude.

"No," Robert answered, matching her attitude. "Foundling is where children born out of wedlock and abandoned children are left. Penda is married, and we will treat her as a married woman since marriage is sacred in the eyes of God regardless of skin color or status."

"A woman who has sunk so low should suffer the consequences. Never look to me to help her. She is a slave. And if this baby lives and is a girl, she should be given my name. If a boy, Matthew, since she is our property."

"Your name is not a Bible name. I learned that you renamed all your slaves with Bible names. Why?"

There was no response to Robert's question.

"What about your plantation records? Would your brother not know where they are?" Robert asked, continuing to match her bristling attitude.

"My brother would know them," she answered weakly.

"Here's what I need from you as soon as possible, a record of the transaction and the ship's records that brought her to England."

Robert remembering her history of mental illness in Barbados, he thought she would not have access to the records or remembered.

"As reimbursement for her care, I will compensate you for the six months she was in your employment since by your admission the girl has received no wages here in England, only compelled to provide hours of unpaid labor."

"Sarah's name is Penda, and she is free here in England. Servants are voluntary and are paid. Since you have no papers for her and you haven't paid her, she is free to leave."

Catherine had no response for him. She remained silent, thinking he should say more, and Robert was silent, thinking he had given her ample time to speak. The silence extended. He then volunteered to get the appropriate document stating the girl was free.

The following week, Robert received a document stating Penda was a free woman.

That evening, Robert sat down with a bottle of wine and told Penda the results of his visits to Catherine, his plan to get her to Lady Avonlea, and the work she was doing in Bristol.

"What you want is here in England. You will have to choose and do what is best for yourself and your baby."

"Thank you for your kindness, Mr. Parker." She shifted in her chair as she searched for words that would be fitting to express her gratitude for how she had been treated.

All she heard herself say was "Thank you for everything."

Penda made plans to be at the wharf the next Friday as set forth in the list in the library. It would be difficult with her big bulge. Early that morning, before Robert got up, Penda made her way to the farm and climbed in the buggy, covering herself, planning to be at the wharf when the ship came. Finding it too uncomfortable, she abandoned the plan and returned to the house. Robert also had a plan not shared with Penda. He would take his housekeeper and Penda to the shops by way of the wharf; it would look like he and his mother had their servant with them.

Initially, he thought of taking the girl alone but was afraid he might be forced to return her to slavery since his abolitionist activity remained secret. He hoped that she would see the slaves/servants as they walked off the ship, and by her reaction, he would know she had recognized Absalom, her husband. He prayed her pregnancy was not further along and no one would offer to buy her.

The dock was busy, hawkers shouted their wares, and barrels rolled noisily over the cobblestones. Men were working on sails and rigging as they shouted at each other. Once, Penda thought she saw him, but when the man turned, she saw he was older than she imagined Kuba would be. Another ship was unloading further down, so Robert moved closer being careful not to go too close to the warehouse where the men and women were going. Down the gangplank walked a line of black men and women walking together with their masters and mistresses.

Penda scanned the line for Kuba. Again, she thought she saw him—another man of similar build—but as he got closer to the buggy, he turned his face away and hung his head down. Unsure and disappointed, she turned away as the tears fell. Tearing her eyes away from the warehouse where the servants and their masters went, her eyes caught the name of the ship, *God's Angel*. In Robert's library was a large picture of a ship named *God's Angel*. Robert stood motionless, horrified, as if an overhanging cloud had lifted. He could not believe that he had treated human beings made in God's image so inhumanely. He stood as the slave trade, in all its horror, became a reality to him. The picture that unfolded, he had seen many times. The voice of his father, when, after his conversion, he felt repelled by the sale of human beings like sugar and rum.

"Father, we are selling them like sugarcane products," Robert told his father one day.

"They are heathen, boy, and most likely to be saved in a Christian country than if they remain in their own primitive village," was his father's response each time. "Or the money earned from slavery has given us a standard of living that is enviable. Land ownership is the defining mark of a gentleman. It confers status and influence."

Resolved to treat blacks the same as whites—a stance that made him unpopular—as merchants discovered Robert's covert crusade against slavery. For a long time Robert continued to stand as if in a trance. Unaware of the stench of the wharf or the stares of people, silently he accepted his disappointment at not finding Penda's husband, so they left the wharf.

Early the next morning, Penda was suddenly awakened by a noise outside her door. As she lay there, she thought now six months had passed; the movements of the baby were strong. *Three months to go*, she thought. *But what can I do?* She had gone by the Foundling Hospital but was turned away. There was a loud knocking on her bedroom door. On opening the door, Robert was standing there.

"Get your things together quickly and come with me" was all he said. She grabbed her Bible and as many clothes as she could push into a bag. He helped her up in the buggy, pulled the cover-up, and they left Downham Farm. Heart thumping, Penda held her hand over her stomach and closed her eyes, holding back tears of fear and relief. During the first half of the journey, Robert remained silent. Rumors and conversations around the village had it that when the black servant at Downham Manor gave birth, the baby would be removed and transferred to a wiser and better guardianship, like the Foundling's, for the guidance of one who has stumbled and fallen—speaking of Penda. It was believed that having an illegitimate child was a badge of shame. To Robert's housekeeper relaying gossip and rumors, Robert said, "The child shall be well cared for if she remains here. God gave the baby into Penda's keeping, and she should not be forced to give her up."

During the quietness, Robert replayed his first sight of a slave auction—the parade of nude females, some of them with babies that were born on the ship in their arms.

"It was greed that made us use color and God to get what we wanted," he concluded. Robert wanted as few people as possible to know of his crusade to free as many slaves as possible. He believed that those who knew hated him. He traveled to London and organized meetings that were aimed at conjoining like-minded people to bring pressure to bear on parliament to change the slave laws. His group comprised lawyers, doctors, and a couple of former slaves who could get away unnoticed. He had been repelled by the slave trade. He had surrendered his life to working for its abolition.

During the silence, Penda recalled an incident that pointed to Catherine's regression. The girl was in the kitchen, setting a tray for her, when the mistress called. On taking the tray, Catherine demanded to know where she was when called. Penda noticed she had become very suspicious watching her. Catherine then launched out into an angry tirade about the girl being saved through her, and she should be thankful for a house to live in.

"Bless this kind man, Lord, and Lady Avonlea," she whispered. "Had it not been for him that wintry night…" she let the words trail off. "You saved me and my baby through this man, who has shown me what the Bible means when it speaks of loving your neighbor as yourself."

Several switches of buggies were made until they reached a very large house surrounded by buildings. There she saw people and a few children that looked like her.

Lady Avonlea lived in Bristol and worked with abolitionists who provided some safe havens. There the former slaves were taught to read, write, and do domestic activities like knitting and sewing. Lady Avonlea welcomed her and, on noticing the bump in her belly, added, "You and your baby may live here. We educate in reading, and we teach skills. After you learn to read and write, I will find a place of employment for you with a Christian master and mistress."

That night over a hearty meal, Lady Avonlea talked a little to Penda, hoping to help her settle. *She spoke to me as a human being her equal*, she thought.

"Robert is much hated for his crusade against slavery."

"His crusade?" Penda asked with a confused look on her face.

"Obviously, you are not aware of his work with the abolitionists against the trade. He travels to London, arranging meetings with like-minded people to pressure parliament to change the laws."

After the meal, she was shown the school and her room. That night, Penda closed her eyes in relief, and she smiled in the darkness. There was no fear or sense of being sold, just an awareness of God's goodness. Her worrying about the baby's well-being when born, she thought, would soon be over.

Early instruction at Lady Avonlea included how to address people. All men whose title she was unsure of would be called sir and all women dame unless she knew her title. Good manners require the avoidance of anything that would offend or inconvenience anyone. Swearing phrases like "oh, for God's sake" or "bloody hell" to express shock should never be spoken. Penda was taught a handshake meant to respect and confirm agreements. On eating, laughter with a mouth full of food was a breach of manners, and she was to chew with her mouth closed when eating. Prayers at the start and end of the meal.

Penda went into labor one Friday night in early November. At first, the pains came at irregular intervals, becoming stronger and more regular throughout the day. By midday, the pains became concentrated in her back.

"Feel as if my back is tearing apart," she told the housekeeper. Lady Avonlea's housekeeper had secured the services of a midwife for Penda's delivery. Mrs. Henry was an older woman who had delivered hundreds of babies in Bristol. Penda thought she would be more at ease with an older, experienced woman. She was happy to learn that the midwife had been sent for as pains were now coming hard and regular. She feared that the baby might come before the midwife arrived. When the midwife arrived, one look at the girl's face confirmed that the baby's arrival was imminent.

"Did the pains start long? she asked, looking at Penda occasionally while setting out things she needed.

"Last night," Penda answered through gritted teeth.

"I should have been called sooner," Mrs. Henry said in a scolding voice. All Penda could concentrate on then was bearing the pain. The room became hot with heat from the fire. Beads of sweat poured; it felt like the pain was everywhere, swallowing her up.

"Is the girl strong enough to deliver this baby?" the housekeeper asked.

"Yes, she can do it," Mrs. Henry assured her. To Penda, she added, "You're doing fine, not much longer now."

"Ma!" Penda shouted, starting to cry for her mother. After what seemed like much feeling and checking internally by the midwife, Penda was instructed to "push now!" Following instructions, Penda pushed over and over. The intensity of the pain moved from her body and became concentrated between her legs.

"You have a girl," a voice said.

Another said, "Take her away."

"No!" she cried. "Give her to me!"

"It's best if they don't hold them or see them, easier to give them up to the Foundling Hospital." This time, she heard a man's voice.

"Who feeds the babies at the hospital?" said the midwife. Penda was back at the plantation, watching the scene unfold.

"No!" Penda cried. "My daughter—I want her." Then a voice shattered her dream, she was in Bristol at Lady Avonlea's farm.

"You have a daughter, Penda," said the midwife. Penda's eyes were fixed on the left side of the room as if seeing someone.

"Come my, daughter," she said with urgency when there was no sound from the infant. There was a hushed silence in the room as they waited to hear the baby cry. After what seemed like a long time, the baby gave a faint whimper.

"The baby should be baptized and given a Christian name," the midwife suggested.

When Penda looked at the baby's little face, her cap of black hair still wet from the moisture of birth, love rose in her. Alongside her joy, she saw a perfect human being that came from her body—innocent and vulnerable—along with a grief and a longing for her husband, Kuba, who she admitted she may never see. Mrs. Henry wanted to clean the baby and lay her in a crib, but Penda refused, fearing she may not be safe. Mrs. Henry dried and wrapped the baby, then handed her to Penda.

She said, "She came quickly for a first baby." When the midwife left the housekeeper, smiling, she said, "She looks healthy. Have you thought of a name for her yet?"

"Yes." She thought of Mammy's firstborn, Aminka, which means strong and persistent. She decided to honor Mammy. "Her name is Aminka."

"How about Susan? That's a nice Christian name," someone suggested.

"No. Aminka."

Penda closed her eyes, listening to the soft steady breathing of the one who had brought such joy and light into her existence. Aminka was asleep. Penda gently lifted her baby from the crib. She put the baby on her chest for the first time holding her close, finding comfort in the innocence of the baby who had no knowledge of doubt or fear.

"I wonder about your future—what will be said over you. Who will you look like, me or your father? What will your world be like? Lord, teach me to trust you like this baby and remember that you know when a sparrow falls. I know you love me more than the sparrow. Watch over this baby, keep her safe." Penda prayed this every morning.

One evening after supper, as Penda was helping to clear the table, Lady Avonlea asked her if she could read and write. "Yes, I can read, but no, I cannot write."

To which her hostess replied, "If you wish to learn to write, I'll ask teacher Martha. We can start on Monday after breakfast." On the agreed day, an assortment of books and slates were brought out and so began Penda's journey of learning to write. She was excited about learning how to make the loops, curves, and lines into words to begin writing. She also felt reassured after meeting a couple of black men and women who worked for Lady Avonlea. For the first two weeks, she practiced writing the letters from the Bible using chalk to make them into words.

Penda's first specimen of handwriting was a letter she penned to Mr. Robert Parker.

> Six months ago, you rescued me one stormy night. I had nowhere to go and knew no one in Lancashire. I was thrown out by my mistress, who thought I was pregnant for her husband. I was a stranger to you and of a different color. As the Bible says, "I was hungry, and you fed me." You helped me to remember my birth name, Penda—a name that slavery had denied me. You saw in me what at the time I could not see—

buried skills and vision of a good future. Thank you for all you have done for me. Because of you, I have accomplished the ability to choose, which is all I ever dreamed of. I will never forget you.

Penda and her daughter were now settled at Lady Avonlea's school. She could write now, shop, and do all the things young women were taught to become good servants. Penda has now lived in Bristol for the past two years, being taught dressmaking. The days were passing quickly. After one year, her teacher Martha, one of the best dressmakers in Bristol, had observed how quickly the girl grasped everything she taught her about sewing. She noted that Penda did not even need to make a paper pattern. She would measure and chalk straight onto the cloth, and the dress would fit. Her sewing was becoming sought-after among the known ladies of the town. Penda completed her orders efficiently though some of the designs for gowns were difficult. Penda was growing more accustomed to the routine of the house and school, yet there were many times when she longed for the familiarity of the plantation.

"What we taught you here was only the beginning of how to write and do basic sewing, but I want you to concentrate on designing and sewing—not just knowing how to stitch two pieces of cloth together but how to make fancy dresses and ball gowns for the ladies."

As the months passed, Aminka's growth was evident. *Hard to believe that she is already one year old today*, Penda thought. She was healthy and had started walking. Bits of Kuba are seen in her features. Every day, Penda prayed, asking God to protect her and the child from those who would want to do them harm.

CHAPTER 4

Penda learned quickly under Lady Avonlea's tutelage. The main aim of the school was good manners, basic reading, and writing, as well as skills like cooking, housework, and needlework.

"It's your gift from God," her teacher would say. "Let's start with making a simple coat."

It was all hand stitching, and by the third week, Penda knew which needle to use with which fabric. She could also do many types of stitches like running stitches, back stitches, and embroidery. Penda did such a good job.

"No one could tell a human hand had done the stitches," her teacher would often remark.

Mrs. Thorpe was a good teacher, and before long, Penda was able to name each fabric with her eyes closed. Just by feeling the fabric, she was able to name gingham, velvet, wool, cotton, silk taffeta, and brocade. Embroidery was her weakest and hardest skill to learn as she had never handled a needle. Next, she had to learn the types of fabrics like silk and lace.

How this all started—one day, a woman came to visit Lady Avonlea. She then visited the school and the classrooms. Leaning over Penda, she asked, "Where did you learn to do such fine work?"

"Here at Lady Avonlea, ma'am," Penda answered. The woman moved a little distance away and stood watching. After what seemed like a long time, she moved on to see the other classes and chat with Mrs. Thorpe, the teacher giving the impression this was her custom.

"How long has the girl been here?" The visitor's voice was overheard asking.

"She has been here for about a year," Mrs. Thorpe replied.

"The last two times I was here, I must have missed her."

"She goes with Lady Avonlea monthly to choose fabrics, trimmings, and threads. You may have come on those Fridays."

A week later, the teacher informed Penda that the lady who examined her work was Mrs. Connolly, a grand lady who visited occasionally to inspect what the school was doing for servants and slaves. After seeing Penda's work, she asked Mrs. Thorpe if she could send her housekeeper to interview Penda about going into her personal service.

"Mrs. Connolly, a grand lady!" Penda was excited but scared too, having never been so close to a lady. Something must have been arranged, because at eleven o'clock the following Friday, Mrs. Connolly's housekeeper arrived. She was a big woman, that is all Penda remembered. The woman asked to see all Penda's work, adding, "You will be sewing for the highest lady in Bristol." "Would she be taking Aminka as well?" Penda asked a question to herself. "What does it mean?"

"Lay all your work out on Mrs. Thorpe's desk," she instructed Penda. Then the questions began: What is the fabric? What needles did you use and what type of thread? Why did you use those stitches? Penda answered as well as she could. Finally, the woman said, "I love what I see."

"Penda is one of our best seamstresses. I think the girl will do nicely," commented Mrs. Thorpe.

"The driver will come to collect her the day after tomorrow."

"Penda has a daughter. What are your mistress's plans for her? Is she aware?"

"She can be taught and gotten ready for service."

Penda did not wish her daughter to be a servant. She had visions of Aminka following in her footsteps, sewing for the grand ladies of Bristol and London and being independent.

In dressmaking, Penda excelled. The immediate consequence of Penda making two exceptionally attractive gowns for Lady Avonlea was that she acquired two wealthy and influential clients. One was Mrs. Margaret Lynch and Lady Wellington; both expressed surprise at the girl's workmanship. Mrs. Lynch was happy with the efficiency with which Penda designed and cut the fabric, admitting that she was often impatient with her during fittings but was satisfied with the finished gown.

"My dear, you are wasting your talent here in Bristol. You could do better in London, making a fortune." She told Penda one day after her fitting. Penda thought about her words but almost immediately canceled them out with the thought, *What of my daughter?*

Penda smiled. "My home is here at Lady Avonlea. The work comes second to my daughter, Aminka." Turning to Lady Avonlea, who was at the final fitting for the gowns, Mrs. Lynch said, "What a waste of such talent. Even allowing for the fact that she has no recognized name, and you live way out here in a remote location. Your servant could charge twice the amount, and it would still be lower than the London prices. You must also teach her to be businesslike."

"I have no understanding of what dressmakers charge, and the girl is not my servant. I am teaching her a skill that she can use to provide for her and her daughter."

"I will get you a scale of charges, and you can modify accordingly." She was unaware that Penda was now reading fluently and understood the English language. Lady Avonlea accepted the scale of charges, horrified at first; eventually, she regulated them, aware of the girl's lack of knowledge and experience with money. Penda was learning but was having challenges with the pounds, shillings, and pence.

"I think you have an exceptional talent, Penda. A woman like Mrs. Lynch would never shout your praise so loudly without good reason, nor would Mrs. Wellington allow a mediocre dressmaker to sew her dresses and gowns."

Lady Avonlea was influenced by the suggested charges and quietly planned to make a little space in her house for the girl to sew. Since word had gone out about her work, she calculated she could make a profit from her hours of lessons. She considered asking one of the girls she taught to help Penda with the dull part of sewing. A day later, Lady Avonlea came to Penda's room.

"I know a girl in the village, Mary, who was schooled here. She works at the convent. I could ask the nuns as I've been told she doesn't like it there, and she could help you with the boring jobs like trimming threads and hemming."

"That would be helpful," Penda answered as she often wished she could avoid the lengthy tasks of hemming and smocking. So Mary started gladly that week. Between work, she let Mary help the housekeeper in the kitchen.

Penda's small but select clientele kept her busy. She had acquired a reputation as a seamstress and dressmaker in a relatively short time. The best ladies in Bristol were her patrons, and when her reputation was established, she never lacked orders. Sewing expensive clothes for the women was difficult to cut and carried a lot of trimming. She felt she had earned her education. She had sat long hours at the sewing machine and had stitched endless hours to perfect side seams, gathering, and tucking. Penda thanked God for the distance he had carried her and for the rest of the journey he promised to complete with her. Then she spent the morning in a state of euphoria, recollecting all the events of her time at Robert's and Lady Avonlea's. She indulged herself in a game of who-would-have-thought. Who would have thought that after just six months in England, I would be thrown out on the streets, searching for help—or that I would be free with papers to support my status? Or that the slave girl who could not read or write on the plantation would be living at Lady Avonlea as an educated woman? Or that I would be sought out for sewing gowns for the upper class? She remembered when embroidery was her hardest skill to learn. She gave thanks to God for his help and watchfulness over her.

Penda remembered the first time the teacher said to her, "Let me see your stitches." Penda had been learning for six months. The school day had ended when the teacher, Mrs. Martha Thorpe, made the request. Penda passed the work to be judged into her hand. Martha studied the needlework carefully, then she said, "You are greatly improved, but you need to remove the stitches from the hem. Some areas are puckered, and the hems need to lay flat. Maybe you are pulling the thread too tight."

Robert visited Lady Avonlea occasionally when he had a slave/servant to place under her tutelage. After Penda's name became a household word in Bristol, Robert went to visit her.

"I have a seat on the parish council and the county council," Robert told her.

Penda had suspected he was in something, for she lived with him. She would overhear him at times telling the housekeeper that he would be catching an early train in the morning as he had a meeting in London or Bristol to attend. After greeting Lady Avonlea, he pulled Penda aside, indicating he needed to speak with her without an audience.

"I intend to stand for parliament and would like you some time to share your plantation experience. He knew that her speech had improved with her reading. Penda gasped, and he smiled.

"How can I or anyone affect important issues unless we have a platform or a voice? I think regular people like you should be given a voice."

Seeing her dumbfounded expression, he laughed and was about to walk away when she responded, "Sir, I would like to go on with my needlework if allowed."

What she really wanted to say was that she wanted her husband with her. That day, she learned that he traveled miles in England, setting up antislavery societies, making speeches, and risking his life as he tried to recruit witnesses who would testify to its horrors.

"I think," said Robert, "that it would be a pity for you to stop doing work that you are obviously good at. It seems you have an exceptional talent, Penda. Women like Lady Wellington and Mrs. Lynch would not sound your praise to me so loudly without good reason."

Penda did not respond. She tried to remain unaffected by what he said. Penda listened to him as he continued talking about his plan to be a parliamentarian and his plans for taking part in country and national affairs. In Robert, the girl saw conviction, power, and confidence. He had shown her that from the first night they met when he told her not to be afraid of him and that he was an honest man. While she looked at him, it was obvious that their minds were diverted to different places, both being silent. When he eventually said goodbye and walked away, she stood looking after him. She felt enormous gratitude to him for his kindness, something she vowed she would never forget.

Penda stood immobile. When she roused herself, she had already come to a decision she would stay at Lady Avonlea if permitted. She did not want to leave her farm just yet. What she needed was a private place to do measuring and fitting so that she could have the women undress down to their corsets. Many of them came with their maids to assist. She prayed daily for the time when she would have her own store and attendants. She acknowledged that she was praying big prayers but told herself that she was praying to a big God.

The thought of working in London remained with Penda. Though now a free woman, the money she earned was scant, and she thought that since no one knew her in London, her sewing may be too inconsistent to enable her the means to set up shop. She would speak with Lady Avonlea about keeping Aminka and continuing her education.

While fitting and dressing Mrs. Connolly another day, the subject of London and being the dressmaker for her and the staff came up.

"Penda, you are so good at dressmaking. Have you considered what I asked you? I will see to it that you are set up, and I will pay you a generous salary."

"Ma'am, you would need to speak to Lady Avonlea about that," she answered quietly. Penda was bewildered by the offer. At first, she was tempted to go with her as her promise seemed reasonable. However, as the days passed, she thought over the invitation a couple of times but felt less inclined after reading about some of the mishaps and treatments of free blacks in London. The accounts came from a newspaper that Lady Avonlea encouraged them to read.

The night after Mrs. Connolly's suggestion, Penda found it impossible to sleep.

"I could accept her suggestion and move to London." She examined the thought from different angles. "Could I really make it in London?"

The thought cheered her up a little, then she reminded herself that she had found her skill in sewing that she loved, and then there was Aminka who was learning and growing well.

She was on her way to the shops one Friday. She had a couple of gowns to finish for the ball that night. Several of the ladies invited wanted Penda to make their dresses.

"Your dress is going to be the best of all the dresses I will make, Lady Avonlea," Penda boasted.

There was a nice breeze. A carriage was drawn up in the shade of a large tree. She had been living in Bristol for the past five years and had become familiar with the shops in the village, especially those that sold stuff for dressmaking. As she walked toward the parade, she meditated on her time in England, evolving ideas for dresses—each visualized as unique and lovely—the progress she had made. She would often pray and give thanks to God for his faithfulness. She still felt somewhat trapped, unable to see herself beyond the status of servant. *Had God gone asleep?* she asked. *No* was her quick reply to herself. "The Bible states he does not take a nap in the day or sleep through the night," she answered. Penda was so lost in her thoughts she did not see the buggy bearing down on her. A butcher's cart loaded with animal carcasses sprang out of an alley, coming toward her.

"Watch out!" It was a man's voice—the shout was commanding, authoritative. She stopped a few inches from the horse's hooves, frozen for a moment. Then recovering herself, she moved on to the row of shops. As she resumed walking, she heard a voice shout "Sarah." The voice came from a black man sitting in a buggy across the lane. The man alighted from the buggy and caught up with her, holding her arm. He asked her name.

"I'm looking for Sarah from Barbados." His eyes were fastened on her in a disbelieving way. Penda stopped, turned to look at him, and got emotional and confused. From the blue uniform he was wearing, Penda knew he was a servant.

Master Thorpe brought a new stable man to Broadhurst Farm who kept talking about a girl named Sarah. "What is your name if not Sarah?" His voice sounded urgent.

"My name is not Sarah," she said, yet her heart was beating wildly as if she should own the name.

"I'm looking for Sarah from Coconut Palms."

Penda snatched her hand away. *Dear Lord*, she thought as panic rose in her. *Kuba?* She kept repeating. She didn't trust this man.

"I must be mistaken," he said as he turned, walked back to his buggy, and drove down the street.

"Did he really know Kuba, or was this a trick?" There was something about his face that resembled the slave catcher in Barbados at Coconut Palms. The slave catcher she knew was old then and would be much older now.

Did he make a mistake? She wanted to know more about the stranger but was afraid it might be a trick. Common sense told her to leave any thought of finding Kuba through him alone. As she walked away, she remembered their midnight parting, how they looked at each other and how they both tearfully accepted that nothing in their lives would ever be the same again. Before Kuba left, he said, "Me find you in England." As she stood watching him run toward the camp, she told herself, "Me going be alright."

For weeks, Penda would replay the meeting with the stranger in her head. She made a vow to herself that if Kuba was in England, she would find him. She knew that Lady Avonlea received servants from the West Indies at her farm. She figured if she offered to clean the library for Lady Avonlea, she would be able to know the comings and goings of new servants. She asked and received permission to help in the library as no one suspected her motive.

Colonel Thorpe from Broadhurst Farm was a regular visitor to Lady Avonlea. He visited weekly for tea. On his last visit, Penda and the housekeeper overheard him describing his latest purchase of a young man named Absolom from Barbados. His plan was to have him work in the stables. Based on the description of the man, Penda thought it could be her husband, Kuba. Upon hearing this, she remembered her last trip to the port with Robert where the man she thought was Kuba turned his face away. The following day, Penda made a startling discovery in the library. She found the list of servants arriving on the ship *Maria* from the Caribbean. It was due to dock in Bristol the following day, Friday, November 28. She clutched the list tightly to her breast, just the faintest possibility of seeing Kuba's face was all Penda desired at that moment.

On Friday evening, Penda made her way to the port just as the sun was casting long shadows over Bristol. She stood a little distance away from the port, positioning herself at a place where she could not be seen by anyone from Lady Avonlea's place who might be there to pick him up, yet close enough to see the passengers as they disembarked. She kept straining her eyes, but there was no sight of Kuba. But just as doubt, hope, and fear began to take up residence in her heart, her pulse quickened as a figure emerged walking down the gangplank. Was it him? Or was she mistaken? As the silhouette came closer, the figure seemed familiar yet obscured by the distance and fading light. The next few steps of the man would either determine it is Kuba or shatter her hope completely. Penda waited, holding her breath as the tall figure of a man walked away from the gangplank toward the warehouse.

CLOSURE

Remembering can be painful sometimes, but I know from experience that it is far preferable to having no memory at all.

The plantation had been my home and cruel master. It took my parents and stole my friends Odon and Kuba. It deprived me of rights and privileges. The plantation taught me skills like how to read, deliver babies, and learn herbs for curing all kinds of ailments. Everyone I knew then is no more. Life in Barbados was cruel, but it is the only life I knew from age fourteen, and now it is finished. The memory of Mammy is always very close, but I have consciously shut the memories of my mother out ages ago. Every day presents an opportunity for me to review one of the lessons she taught me at Coconut Palms. In my eyes, Mammie was a woman who in another world would have been great. She taught me about the written word of the Bible when slave laws prohibited slaves from learning to read or write.

"Get out!" are the first English words I learned at Coconut Palms. Words shouted after a conch shell blew just before daybreak. Men, women, and children assembled quickly following the words that announced the beginning of another workday.

Barbados and England have lived on in my memory, so have my capture, the long walk, the overcrowded and unsanitary conditions on the boat, my sale and loss of identity, the branding the cruelty… girls like Esther, as soon as they become women planters and overseers take them to their beds or the shed. No one is standing up for them. Sometimes remembering can be painful and distressing, but I know from experience, it is preferable to having no memory at all. I am free to remember my village and the villagers dancing to the beat of the drums. I know the village is no longer there, but I rebuilt it in my memory. The clear moon, the long grass around the compound, my mud house, earthen pots, and the fears I had of offending my ancestors. From the door of my hut, I could see the hills and experience the rainy season. I marvel at how a tree shoots up during the rainy season where there is only a small crack in the mud. The village had lots of anthills. What I lost in my memory, I can recover and build in my mind. Any reminders or images of the plantation my mind brings up, I shove to the past because I know slavery was about money.

Hard to believe that I am the fourteen-year-old girl who survived the slave ship and made it to Barbados. Now I am here in England. Born in a village hut in Karembe territory along the Kwango river. My tribal name at birth was Penda, meaning *she who is loved*. I am now eighteen or nineteen years old, worn by work and lack of care. My hands and feet are hardened, and my breasts droop. I was a happy youth before capture, now my expression I know has become somber. I do not know the day, month, or year when I was born, but when captured, I was fourteen yam seasons. One day I'm a slave, with no legal rights, and today I'm in England as a servant with no legal rights. I can read and write. My name is no longer Sarah, slave of Mapp. I lost more than my relatives when I was taken, and I lost a part of my identity.

As slaves, we were a group of people originally from different countries in Africa. We walked off the slave ships and were forced to adopt different identities. I became Sarah, slave of Mapp. Had I remained on the plantation, there, my identity as a slave would have remained permanent even to any children I had. The things I have seen, the things I have survived, the capture, the long walk of weeks to the coast, the stories I told myself to remain sane. The horrors of the ship, the stench, the nakedness, men, and women leaping overboard into the mouths of sharks. Many deaths were witnessed on the way to Barbados, and many died at Coconut Palms. I have no more tears to shed. My clothing has changed for the better. I no longer wear old clothes or ill-fitting faded dresses for my uniform. My initial assessment of England was that it was damp and foggy most of the year and to see the sun was a treat.

There is the memory of Kuba who came to spend the night with me the day before I was scheduled to leave the plantation. I awaited my last day on the plantation with a sense of hope and hopelessness. It's a journey where my choices were not considered, something I could do nothing about. The decision had been made for me, not of my own volition, treated as someone without will. As day approaches, I watch him leave while it is still dark. I feel guilty and sad at the same time, but I'm using the teachings of Mammy and the Bible to help me make the transition though difficult at times, to a new way of life and thinking. Exposure to the British culture has further weakened the connection I had with my tribal past.

I know It's God's faithfulness and vigilance that has spared me from the horror of being raped or used as a breeder. Master Mapp once overheard saying to Bassa, "A barren gal isn't worth one penny."

I'm happy he never checked my fertility status. This is not a subject Preacher Brown talked about. I get embarrassed whenever I recall the times Mammie read from the Bible, a book as far as I was concerned could have been a piece of wood. I was illiterate. Couldn't read the letters mistress left opened knowing that they may have contained a date for my sale or return to Barbados. I couldn't read.

The night of the storm, Kuba did not think of himself or the risk of being captured. I have tucked away this strange yet precious memory, alongside that of Mammy. I want Kuba and myself to experience freedom together. I want us to be a family since learning that the Bible says, "What God has joined together, let no man put apart." What I long for is a world where fathers and mothers are not forcibly separated from their children by masters and mistresses, and they live under one roof as we did in Lunda. Not as many women on the plantation were forced to marry a man chosen by the master, I want to believe that here in England I am free to love.

As a slave, no one saw my vulnerability or my need for people. There is so much about the meaning of freedom that I am yet to learn like the ability to choose who touches my body or to make independent decisions. As slaves, we were unable to carry out the normal duties of a parent or even to become a woman naturally as God intended. Many of the young children on the plantation did not know their mothers or fathers if they were bought from another plantation. The Bible speaks of "when I was a child, I thought as a child, I reasoned as a child. When I became a man..." sadly that phrase never became a reality in the men's lives, who seemed doomed to remain boy or other derogatory title all their lives.

To some people, slavery was a good thing, it introduced us the heathens to Jesus,' but it kept me from having a home and a husband who became a man as a runaway.

I was prohibited from forming relationships, by deliberately choosing us from different villages, making us unable to communicate; even God said, "Come, let us reason together." If God wants us to communicate, it must have some meaning to him. As I look back at the system of slavery, I see that my whole life of working, learning, and loving was rigidly controlled by slave laws that restricted me from living a normal life; like playing with a baby or holding them. The Bible says that "we are free in Christ," yet the Bible was a sealed book to us.

Freedom is bought at a price. Birds prefer to fly among the trees, in the woods, and even in all kinds of weather as opposed to being in a golden cage with abundant pampering. Where I once feared slavery thinking it was sent to destroy me, now I believe it was a messenger God sent to bring me freedom, for without sugar, I would not have been introduced to Mammy or her God.

On an island where people of my color were in the majority but not the ruling class, it was impossible to form any sense of my value as a human being; for example, using our breasts to feed the babies of our English slavers. We are forced to adopt the ways of the planters, learn their language by the whip, and forget who we are.

The hereditary character of slavery struck me hard when I learned that a father who is a slave when he dies leaves nothing but toil for his children, nothing, but his place on the palette in the corner of the hut and his children leave the same to their offspring.

Strange now as I look back that we were chosen or priced according to the firmness and perceived strength of our body and how well we would endure degradation, neglect, and ill-treatment. To overhear, it said of us, "They care for nothing."

I have a Bible, one that I got from Mammie when she died. I read it every day, I find words like, "Trust in the Lord with all thine heart and lean not to your own understanding in all your ways acknowledge him and He shall direct your paths."

Marriage, I consider a blessing designed for the free to choose, yet it was only used with the slaves to perpetuate the system.

Preacher Brown would come every Sunday, place stress on the word obedience, and be grateful for all our blessings. I think of his repeated sermons on "love your masters, obey them, serve them faithfully, it is pleasing in the sight of your heavenly Father." We were happiest on Sundays when we would sing and shout and make up songs to replace the hymns that only he could read and sing. I knew that the time of singing and shouting could not sustain our broken spirits throughout the week of working sunrise to sunset and beyond on some days, under the constant fear of the whip.

Was Preacher Brown a hypocrite? Did he believe what he preached? Or did he not know that we were starved, or about the quiet grieving mothers who had the children torn from their arms and sold or of the young women forced into immoral filth or did he not see blood around the whipping posts? How did he conduct the funerals? I know now that there is a big difference between Christianity and religion. After I learned to read, I found in the Bible where the apostle Paul in Ephesians, after he instructs to love masters, he says, "Not with eye service as men pleasers but as bondservants of Christ." A bit further on, I read, "You, masters, do the same things to them, giving up threatening, because there is no partiality with God." This gave me calm. Thankful I could read. No one can hide the truth from me any longer. The plantation without God taught me I would never amount to anything but a slave, but as I grew older, I learned from the Bible that faith, hope, and love were not relegated to any one race but universal.

On education, I am thankful for Mammy taking the time to teach me to read. She became my mother, teacher, and friend. Learning to read the Bible was not all she taught me, she shared insights, morals, and what it means to be a true servant of God. I knew that if my ability to read was discovered, I could be sold; masters did not permit or encourage it unless it helped them. I once heard mistress tell the governor that educating us would make us less subservient to the mistresses and masters, and we were not ever to be seen as men and women, but in the same light as domestic animals.

I have learned that nothing in life is permanent. I also learned that slavery was not confined to Coconut Palms plantation, but it's wherever people were shackled to something that controlled them in this case it was money.

As I think of the life of a child and reflect on the way life on Coconut Palms banished those automatic things of a childlike kindness and innocence, I shudder. The only thing they knew was loss and sorrow by the time they had reached five or six.

Regarding religion, initially I wish I could have believed in God like Mammie did, but the blatant disregard for humanity that existed on the plantation affected me more than a desire to know God. I'm happy I learned under Mammy's tutelage that my value as a person is not determined by my status as a slave or a servant but by you, Lord, who created me.

There is no education like adversity. I have derived more benefit, inner strength, and growth from my life as a slave than if I had remained in Lunda. I have come to believe that troubles have a way of removing our rust.

While living at Robert Parker's house I found it interesting that, a man who was once a slaver was taking good care of me. He provided me with food and shelter. Now I have clothes that fit and keep me warm. My bed is a bed no longer a mat on the cold damp floor. I wanted to trust him but knew that the trust that was destroyed would take time to be restored. To trust is to become vulnerable. There are some things I do not wish to remember, like being thrown out. I want to shut them out and make them believe they never happened. Sometimes my mind helps me by blurring them. I'm not alone, for God has made me a promise that he would never leave me, Almighty God, not a mere man. Mammie was right, I must remain focused on what is true and honest and not on the threatening fears of what-ifs.

I have much to be thankful for, most of all a better understanding of who God is through His word. My prayer is that Kuba will know his daughter. I don't know how God will do it, but I have confidence He will see me through, and no matter what the challenge may be I'm confident He will fix it for me.

ABOUT THE AUTHOR

Valdene Williams is a registered nurse with over five decades of experience in the profession. She exemplifies compassion and commitment to maternal women. Her desire to see the world led her to study all aspects of nursing in England. She has written many articles for *The Winepress*, a distinguished publication in the UK. Valdene is also a facilitator of a women's empowerment group, Born to Reign. Her gatherings serve as places for empowering women to discover and own their own uniqueness, destiny, and God's plan for their lives.

    Her life in healthcare has not been confined to the UK and USA. It has taken her on many missionary journeys to Rwanda, Gambia, and Uganda. At home, she is a devoted wife and proud mother of three accomplished adult children.

Printed in the USA
CPSIA information can be obtained
at www.ICGtesting.com
LVHW091928271024
794899LV00003B/549